ABRIDGED CLASSICS

THE GREAT GATSBY

Written by
F. Scott Fitzgerald

Abridged by
Sonal Talwar

Illustrated by
Tanoy Choudhury

Contents

Pre-Reading Activities 3

1. Chapter 1 4
2. Chapter 2 20
3. Chapter 3 30
4. Chapter 4 43
5. Chapter 5 61
6. Chapter 6 78
7. Chapter 7 93
8. Chapter 8 118
9. Chapter 9 141

Post-Reading Activities 160

Pre-Reading Activities

Discuss

1. What do you know about Jazz Age America?

Writing

2. What do you understand by the term 'American Dream' in 1920s?

3. Write about the different strata of American society at that time.

4. Some people think that having money leads to happiness. Do you agree?

5. Have you ever wanted to relive a moment from your past? Describe the situation. How and why would you change the past?

Chapter 1

In my younger and more vulnerable years my father gave me some advice that I've been turning over in my mind ever since.

"Whenever you feel like criticizing any one," he told me, "just remember that all the people in this world haven't had the advantages that you've had."

In consequence I'm inclined to reserve all judgments, a habit that has opened up many curious natures to me and also made me the victim of not a few veteran bores.

When I came back from the East last autumn I felt that I wanted the world to be in uniform and at a sort of moral attention forever.

Only Gatsby, the man who gives his name to this book, was exempt from my reaction, Gatsby who represented everything for which I have an unaffected scorn.

If personality is an unbroken series of successful gestures, then there was something gorgeous about him, some heightened sensitivity to the promises of life.

My family has been prominent, well-to-do people in this middle-western city for three generations.

The Carraways are something of a clan and we have a tradition that we're descended from

Nick Carraway

the Dukes of Buccleuch. But the actual founder of my line was my grandfather's brother who came here in fifty-one, sent a substitute to the Civil War and started the wholesale hardware business that my father carries on today.

I graduated from New Haven in 1915, just a quarter of a century after my father, and a little later I participated in that delayed Teutonic migration known as the Great War.

I enjoyed the counter-raid so thoroughly that I came back restless. Instead of being the warm center of the world the middle-west now seemed like the ragged edge of the universe—so I decided to go east and learn the bond business.

Father agreed to finance me for a year and after various delays I came east, permanently, I thought, in the spring of twenty-two.

The practical thing was to find rooms in the city but it was a warm season and I had just left a country of wide lawns and friendly trees, so when a young man at the office suggested that we take a house together in a commuting town it sounded like a great idea.

He found the house, a weather beaten cardboard bungalow at eighty a month, but at the last minute the firm ordered him to Washington and I went out to the country alone.

I had a dog, at least I had him for a few days until he ran away, and an old Dodge and a Finnish woman who made my bed and cooked breakfast.

It was lonely for a day or so until one morning some man, more recently arrived than I, stopped me on the road.

"How do you get to West Egg village?" he asked helplessly.

I told him. And as I walked on I was lonely no longer. I was a guide, a pathfinder, an original settler.

At West Egg lived those people who have recently become rich and lack an established social position.

On the other hand, East Egg is home to the insular, narrow-minded denizens of the old aristocracy.

I lived at West Egg. My house was at the very tip of the egg, only fifty yards from the Sound, and squeezed between two huge places that rented for twelve or fifteen thousand a season.

The one on my right was an imitation of some Hôtel de Ville in Normandy, with a tower on one side, spanking new under a thin beard of raw ivy, and a marble swimming pool and more than forty acres of lawn and garden.

It was Gatsby's mansion.

Or rather, as I didn't know Mr. Gatsby it was a mansion inhabited by a gentleman of that name.

Across the courtesy bay the white palaces of fashionable East Egg glittered along the water.

I drove over there to have dinner with the Tom Buchanans. Daisy was my second cousin once removed and I'd known Tom in college.

And just after the war I spent two days with them in Chicago.

Her husband, among various physical accomplishments, had been one of the most powerful ends that ever played football at New Haven.

Why they came east I don't know. They had spent a year in France, for no particular reason, and then drifted here and there unrestfully wherever people played polo and were rich together.

This was a permanent move, said Daisy over the telephone, but I didn't believe it.

And so it happened that on a warm windy evening I drove over to East Egg to see two old friends whom I scarcely knew at all.

Their house was even more elaborate than I expected, a cheerful red and white Georgian Colonial mansion overlooking the bay. Tom Buchanan in riding clothes was standing with his legs apart on the front porch.

He changed since his New Haven years.

Now he was a sturdy, straw haired man of thirty with a rather hard mouth and a supercilious manner.

Two shining, arrogant eyes had established dominance over his face and gave him the appearance of always leaning aggressively forward.

Gatsby's Mansion

His speaking voice, a gruff husky tenor, added to the impression of fractiousness he conveyed. We talked for a few minutes on the sunny porch.

"I've got a nice place here," he said, his eyes flashing about restlessly.

Turning me around by one arm he moved a broad flat hand along the front vista, including in its sweep a sunken Italian garden, a half acre of deep pungent roses and a snub-nosed motor boat that bumped the tide off shore.

"It belonged to Demaine the oil man." He turned me around again, politely and abruptly. "We'll go inside."

We walked through a high hallway into a bright rosy-colored space, fragilely bound into the house by French windows at either end.

The windows were ajar and gleaming white against the fresh grass outside that seemed to grow a little way into the house. I must have stood for a few moments listening to the whip and snap of the curtains and the groan of a picture on the wall.

Then there was a boom as Tom Buchanan shut the rear windows and the caught wind died out about the room and the curtains and the rugs and the two young women ballooned slowly to the floor.

The younger of the two was a stranger to me. She was extended full length at her end of the divan, completely motionless and with her chin raised a little as if she were balancing something on it which was quite likely to fall. She was Jordan Baker.

The other girl, Daisy, made an attempt to rise — she leaned slightly forward with a conscientious expression — then she laughed, an absurd, charming little laugh, and I laughed too and came forward into the room.

"I'm p-paralyzed with happiness."

She laughed again, as if she said something very witty, and held my hand for a moment, looking up into my face, promising that there was no one in the world she so much wanted to see.

I told her how I had stopped off in Chicago for a day on my way east and how a dozen people had sent their love through me.

"Do they miss me?" she cried ecstatically.

"The whole town is desolate. All the cars have the left rear wheel painted black as a mourning wreath and there's a persistent wail all night along the North Shore."

"How gorgeous! Let's go back, Tom. Tomorrow!" Then she added irrelevantly, "You ought to see the baby."

"I'd like to."

"She's asleep. She's two years old. Haven't you ever seen her?"

"Never."

"Well, you ought to see her. She's— —"

Nick meets Daisy and Jordan

Tom Buchanan who had been hovering restlessly about the room stopped and rested his hand on my shoulder.

"What you doing, Nick?"

"I'm a bond man."

"Who with?"

I told him.

"Never heard of them," he remarked decisively.

This annoyed me.

"You will," I answered shortly. "You will if you stay in the East."

"Oh, I'll stay in the East, don't you worry," he said, glancing at Daisy and then back at me, as if he were alert for something more.

"I'd be a God Damned fool to live anywhere else."

At this point Miss Baker said "Absolutely!" with such suddenness that I started—it was the first word she uttered since I came into the room.

Evidently it surprised her as much as it did me, for she yawned and with a series of rapid, deft movements stood up into the room.

"I'm stiff," she complained, "I've been lying on that sofa for as long as I can remember."

"Don't look at me," Daisy retorted. "I've been trying to get you to New York all afternoon."

"No, thanks," said Miss Baker to the four cocktails just in from the pantry, "I'm absolutely in training."

Her host looked at her incredulously.

"You are!" He took down his drink as if it were a drop in the bottom of a glass. "How you ever get anything done is beyond me."

I looked at Miss Baker wondering what it was she "got done." I enjoyed looking at her.

She was a slender, small-breasted girl, with an erect carriage which she accentuated by throwing her body backward at the shoulders like a young cadet.

Her grey sun-strained eyes looked back at me with polite reciprocal curiosity out of a wan, charming discontented face. It occurred to me now that I had seen her, or a picture of her, somewhere before.

"You live in West Egg," she remarked contemptuously. "I know somebody there."

"I don't know a single——"

"You must know Gatsby."

"Gatsby?" demanded Daisy. "What Gatsby?"

Before I could reply that he was my neighbor dinner was announced.

"We ought to plan something," yawned Miss Baker, sitting down at the table as if she were getting into bed.

"All right," said Daisy. "What'll we plan?" She turned to me helplessly.

"What do people plan?"

"You make me feel uncivilized, Daisy," I confessed on my second glass of corky but rather impressive claret. "Can't you talk about crops or something?"

I meant nothing in particular by this remark but it was taken up in an unexpected way.

"Civilization's going to pieces," broke out Tom violently.

"I've gotten to be a terrible pessimist about things. Have you read

'The Rise of the Coloured Empires' by this man Goddard?"

"Why, no," I answered, rather surprised by his tone.

"Well, it's a fine book, and everybody ought to read it. The idea is if we don't look out the white race will be—will be utterly submerged.

It's all scientific stuff; it's been proved."

"Tom's getting very profound," said Daisy with an expression of unthoughtful sadness.

"Well, these books are all scientific," insisted Tom, glancing at her impatiently.

Daisy teases Tom about the book. But when Tom leaves the room to take a phone call, Daisy follows him. In the meantime Jordan tells Nick that the call is from Tom's lover in New York.

When Tom leaves the room to take a phone call, Daisy follows him

"Ten o'clock," Baker remarked, apparently finding the time on the ceiling.

"Time for this good girl to go to bed."

"Jordan's going to play in the tournament tomorrow," explained Daisy, "over at Westchester."

"Oh,—you're Jordan Baker."

I knew now why her face was familiar.

"Good night," she said softly. "Wake me at eight, won't you."

"If you'll get up."

"I will. Good night, Mr. Carraway. See you anon."

"Of course you will," confirmed Daisy. "In fact I think I'll arrange a marriage. Come over often, Nick, and I'll sort of—oh—fling you together. You know—lock you up accidentally in linen closets and push you out to sea in a boat, and all that sort of thing——"

"Good night," called Miss Baker from the stairs. "I haven't heard a word."

"She's a nice girl," said Tom after a moment. "They oughtn't to let her run around the country this way."

"Who oughtn't to?" inquired Daisy coldly.

"Her family."

"Her family is one aunt about a thousand years old. Besides, Nick's going to look after her, aren't you, Nick? She's going to spend lots of week-ends out here this summer. I think the home influence will be very good for her."

Daisy and Tom looked at each other for a moment in silence.

"Is she from New York?" I asked quickly.

"From Louisville. Our white girlhood was passed together there. Our beautiful white— —"

"Did you give Nick a little heart to heart talk on the veranda?" demanded Tom suddenly.

"Did I?" She looked at me. "I can't seem to remember, but I think we talked about the Nordic race. Yes, I'm sure we did. It sort of crept up on us and first thing you know— —"

"Don't believe everything you hear, Nick," he advised me.

I said lightly that I had heard nothing at all, and a few minutes later

I got up to go home.

Already it was deep summer on roadhouse roofs and in front of wayside garages, where new red gas-pumps sat out in pools of light, and when I reached my estate at West Egg I ran the car under its shed and sat for a while on an abandoned grass roller in the yard.

The silhouette of a moving cat wavered across the moonlight and turning my head to watch it I saw that I was not alone.

Fifty feet away a figure emerged from the shadow of my neighbour's mansion and was standing with his hands in his pockets regarding the silver pepper of the stars.

Something in his leisurely movements and the secure position of his feet upon the lawn suggested that it was Mr. Gatsby himself, come out to determine what share was his of our local heavens.

Involuntarily I glanced seaward—and distinguished nothing except a single green light, minute and far away, that might have been the end of a dock.

When I looked once more for Gatsby he vanished, and I was alone again in the unquiet darkness.

Chapter 2

About half way between West Egg and New York the motor-road hastily joins the railroad and runs beside it for a quarter of a mile, so as to shrink away from a certain desolate area of land. This is a valley of ashes—a fantastic farm where ashes grow like wheat into ridges and hills.

Above the grey land and the spasms of bleak dust which drift endlessly over it, you perceive, after a moment, the eyes of Doctor T. J. Eckleburg.

The eyes of Doctor T. J. Eckleburg are blue and gigantic—their retinas are one yard high.

The valley of ashes is bounded on one side by a small foul river, and when the drawbridge is up to let barges through, the passengers on waiting trains can stare at the dismal scene for as long as half an hour.

There is always a halt there of at least a minute and it was because of this that I first met Tom Buchanan's mistress.

I went up to New York with Tom on the train one afternoon and when we stopped by the ashheaps he jumped to his feet and taking hold of my elbow literally forced me from the car.

"We're getting off!" he insisted. "I want you to meet my girl."

Tom forces Nick out of the car

I followed him over a low white-washed railroad fence and we walked back a hundred yards along the road under Doctor Eckleburg's persistent stare.

The only building in sight was a small block of yellow brick sitting on the edge of the waste land, a sort of compact Main Street ministering to it and contiguous to absolutely nothing.

One of the three shops it contained was for rent and another was an all-night restaurant approached by a trail of ashes; the third was a garage—Repairs. GEORGE B. WILSON. Cars Bought and Sold—and I followed Tom inside.

"Hello, Wilson, old man," said Tom, slapping him jovially on the shoulder. "How's business?"

"I can't complain," answered Wilson unconvincingly. "When are you going to sell me that car?"

"Next week; I've got my man working on it now."

Tom glanced impatiently around the garage. Then

I heard footsteps on a stairs and in a moment the thickish figure of a woman blocked out the light from the office door.

She was in the middle thirties, and faintly stout, but she carried her surplus flesh sensuously as some women can.

Her face, above a spotted dress of dark blue crepe-de-chine, contained no facet or gleam of beauty but there was an immediately perceptible vitality about her as if the nerves of her body were continually smouldering.

She smiled slowly and walking through her husband as if he were a ghost shook hands with Tom, looking him flush in the eye.

Then she wet her lips and without turning around spoke to her husband in a soft, coarse voice:

"Get some chairs, why don't you, so somebody can sit down."

"Oh, sure," agreed Wilson hurriedly and went toward the little office, mingling immediately with the cement color of the walls.

A white ashen dust veiled his dark suit and his pale hair as it veiled everything in the vicinity— except his wife, who moved close to Tom.

"I want to see you," said Tom intently. "Get on the next train."

"All right."

"I'll meet you by the news-stand on the lower level."

She nodded and moved away from him just as George Wilson emerged with two chairs from his office door.

We waited for her down the road and out of sight. It was a few days before the 4th of July, and a grey, scrawny Italian child was setting torpedoes in a row along the railroad track.

Nick looks at Myrtle

"Terrible place, isn't it," said Tom, exchanging a frown with Doctor Eckleburg.

"Awful."

"It does her good to get away."

"Doesn't her husband object?"

"Wilson? He thinks she goes to see her sister in New York. He's so dumb he doesn't know he's alive."

So Tom Buchanan and his girl and I went up together to New York.

At 158th Street the cab stopped at one slice in a long white cake of apartment houses.

Throwing a regal homecoming glance around the neighbourhood, Mrs. Wilson gathered up her dog and her other purchases and went haughtily in.

The apartment was on the top floor—a small living room, a small dining room, a small bedroom and a bath.

The living room was crowded to the doors with a set of tapestried furniture entirely too large for it. Mrs. Wilson was first concerned with the dog.

A reluctant elevator boy went for a box full of straw and some milk to which he added on his own initiative a tin of large hard dog biscuits—one of which decomposed apathetically in the saucer of milk all afternoon.

Meanwhile Tom brought out a bottle of whiskey from a locked bureau door.

I have been drunk just twice in my life and the second time was that afternoon so everything that happened has a dim hazy cast over it although until after eight o'clock the apartment was full of cheerful sun.

Sitting on Tom's lap Mrs. Wilson called up several people on the telephone; then there were no cigarettes and I went out to buy some at the drug store on the corner. When I came back they had disappeared.

Just as Tom and Myrtle-reappeared, company commenced to arrive at the apartment door.

The sister, Catherine, was a slender, worldly girl of about thirty with a solid sticky bob of red hair and a complexion powdered milky white.

When she moved about there was an incessant clicking as innumerable pottery bracelets jingled up and down upon her arms.

She came in with such a proprietary haste and looked around so possessively at the furniture that I wondered if she lived here.

But when I asked her she laughed immoderately, repeated my question aloud and told me she lived with a girl friend at a hotel.

Mr. McKee was a pale feminine man from the flat below. He informed me that he was in the "artistic game" and I gathered later that he was a photographer.

His wife was shrill, languid, handsome and horrible. She told me with pride that her husband had photographed her a hundred and twenty-seven times since they had been married.

The sister Catherine sat down beside me on the couch.

"Do you live down on Long Island, too?" she inquired.

"I live at West Egg."

"Really? I was down there at a party about a month ago. At a man named Gatsby's. Do you know him?"

"I live next door to him."

"Well, they say he's a nephew or a cousin of Kaiser Wilhelm's. That's where all his money comes from."

"Really?"

She nodded.

The party went on.

It was nine o'clock—almost immediately afterward I looked at my watch and found it was ten.

Mr. McKee was asleep on a chair with his fists clenched in his lap, like a photograph of a man of action.

Taking out my handkerchief I wiped from his cheek the remains of the spot of dried lather that had worried me all the afternoon.

An elevator boy comes to Mrs. Wilson

The little dog was sitting on the table looking with blind eyes through the smoke and from time to time groaning faintly.

People disappeared, reappeared, made plans to go somewhere, and then lost each other, searched for each other, found each other a few feet away.

Some time toward midnight Tom Buchanan and Mrs. Wilson stood face to face discussing in impassioned voices whether Mrs. Wilson had any right to mention Daisy's name.

"Daisy! Daisy! Daisy!" shouted Mrs. Wilson. "I'll say it whenever I want to! Daisy! Dai— —"

Making a short deft movement Tom Buchanan broke her nose with his open hand.

Then there were bloody towels upon the bathroom floor, and women's voices scolding, and high over the confusion a long broken wail of pain.

I left and was staring at the morning "Tribune" and waiting for the four o'clock train.

Chapter 3

There was music from my neighbour's house through the summer nights. In his blue gardens men and girls came and went like moths among the whisperings and the champagne and the stars. I believe that on the first night I went to Gatsby's house I was one of the few guests who had actually been invited. People were not invited—they went there.

Dressed up in white flannels I went over to his lawn a little after seven and wandered around rather ill-at-ease among swirls and eddies of people I didn't know.

As soon as I arrived I made an attempt to find my host but the two or three people of whom I asked his whereabouts denied any knowledge of his movements.

I was on my way to get roaring drunk when

Jordan Baker came out of the house and stood at the head of the marble steps, leaning a little backward and looking with contemptuous interest down into the garden.

"Hello!" I roared, advancing toward her.

"I thought you might be here," she responded absently as I came up.

"I remembered you lived next door to——"

The first supper—there would be another one after midnight—was now being served, and Jordan invited me to join her own party who were spread around a table on the other side of the garden.

"Let's get out," whispered Jordan, after a somehow wasteful and inappropriate half hour. "This is much too polite for me."

We got up, and she explained that we were going to find the host—I had never met him, she said, and it was making me uneasy. The undergraduate nodded in a cynical, melancholy way.

The bar, where we glanced first, was crowded but Gatsby was not there.

She couldn't find him from the top of the steps, and he wasn't on the veranda. On a chance we tried an important-looking door, and walked into a high Gothic library, panelled with carved English oak, and probably transported complete from some ruin overseas.

A stout, middle-aged man with enormous owl-eyed spectacles was sitting somewhat drunk on the edge of a great table, staring with unsteady concentration at the shelves of books. As we entered he wheeled excitedly around and examined Jordan from head to foot.

"What do you think?" he demanded impetuously.

"About what?"

32 F. SCOTT FITZGERALD

Nick and Jordan in the library

He waved his hand toward the book-shelves.

"About that. As a matter of fact you needn't bother to ascertain. I ascertained. They're real."

"The books?"

He nodded.

"Who brought you?" he demanded. "Or did you just come? I was brought.

Most people were brought."

Jordan looked at him alertly, cheerfully without answering.

"I was brought by a woman named Roosevelt," he continued. "Mrs. Claud

Roosevelt. Do you know her?"

"A little bit, I think. I can't tell yet. I've only been here an hour. Did I tell you about the books? They're real. They're——"

"You told us."

We shook hands with him gravely and went back outdoors.

There was dancing now on the canvas in the garden. I was still with Jordan Baker. We were sitting at a table with a man of about my age and a rowdy little girl who gave way upon the slightest provocation to uncontrollable laughter. I was enjoying myself now. I had taken two finger bowls of champagne and the scene had changed before my eyes into something significant, elemental and profound.

At a lull in the entertainment the man looked at me and smiled.

"Your face is familiar," he said, politely. "Weren't you in the Third Division during the war?"

"Why, yes. I was in the Ninth Machine-Gun Battalion."

"I was in the Seventh Infantry until June nineteen-eighteen. I knew I'd seen you somewhere before."

We talked for a moment about some wet, grey little villages in France.

Evidently he lived in this vicinity for he told me that he had just bought a hydroplane and was going to try it out in the morning.

"Want to go with me, old sport? Just near the shore along the Sound."

"What time?"

"Any time that suits you best."

It was on the tip of my tongue to ask his name when Jordan looked around and smiled.

"Having a gay time now?" she inquired.

"Much better." I turned again to my new acquaintance. "This is an unusual party for me. I haven't even seen the host. I live over there——" I waved my hand at the invisible hedge in the distance, "and this man Gatsby sent over his chauffeur with an invitation."

For a moment he looked at me as if he failed to understand.

"I'm Gatsby," he said suddenly.

"What!" I exclaimed. "Oh, I beg your pardon."

"I thought you knew, old sport. I'm afraid I'm not a very good host."

He smiled understandingly—much more than understandingly. It was one of those rare smiles with a quality of eternal reassurance in it, that you may come across four or five times in life.

Almost at the moment when Mr. Gatsby identified himself a butler hurried toward him with the information that Chicago was calling him on the wire. He excused himself with a small bow that included each of us in turn.

"If you want anything just ask for it, old sport," he urged me.

"Excuse me. I will rejoin you later."

When he was gone I turned immediately to Jordan—constrained to assure her of my surprise. I had expected that Mr. Gatsby would be a florid and corpulent person in his middle years.

"Who is he?" I demanded. "Do you know?"

"He's just a man named Gatsby."

"Where is he from, I mean? And what does he do?"

Gatsby in the party

"Now YOU're started on the subject," she answered with a wan smile.

"Well,—he told me once he was an Oxford man."

A dim background started to take shape behind him but at her next remark it faded away.

"However, I don't believe it."

"Why not?"

"I don't know," she insisted, "I just don't think he went there."

There was the boom of a bass drum, and the voice of the orchestra leader rang out suddenly above the echolalia of the garden.

"Ladies and gentlemen," he cried. "At the request of Mr. Gatsby we are going to play for you Mr. Vladimir Tostoff's latest work which attracted so much attention at Carnegie Hall last May. If you read the papers you know there was a big sensation." He smiled with jovial condescension and added "Some sensation!" whereupon everybody laughed.

"The piece is known," he concluded lustily, "as 'Vladimir Tostoff's

Jazz History of the World.' "

Gatsby's butler was suddenly standing beside us.

"Miss Baker?" he inquired. "I beg your pardon but Mr. Gatsby would like to speak to you alone."

"With me?" she exclaimed in surprise.

"Yes, madame."

She got up slowly, raising her eyebrows at me in astonishment, and followed the butler towards the house.

I was alone and it was almost two.

As I waited for my hat in the hall the door of the library opened and

Jordan Baker and Gatsby came out together. He was saying some last word to her but the eagerness in his manner tightened abruptly into formality as several people approached him to say goodbye.

"I've just heard the most amazing thing," she whispered. "How long were we in there?"

"Why,—about an hour."

"It was—simply amazing," she repeated abstractedly. "But I swore

I wouldn't tell it and here I am tantalizing you." She yawned gracefully in my face. "Please come and see me.... Phone book.

... Under the name of Mrs. Sigourney Howard... . My aunt...."

She was hurrying off as she talked—her brown hand waved a jaunty salute as she melted into her party at the door.

Rather ashamed that on my first appearance I had stayed so late, I joined the last of Gatsby's guests who were clustered around him.

I wanted to explain that I'd hunted for him early in the evening and to apologize for not having known him in the garden.

"Don't mention it," he enjoined me eagerly. "Don't give it another thought, old sport." The familiar expression held no more familiarity than the hand which reassuringly brushed my shoulder. "And don't forget we're going up in the hydroplane tomorrow morning at nine o'clock."

Then the butler, behind his shoulder:

"Philadelphia wants you on the phone, sir."

"All right, in a minute. Tell them I'll be right there. . . . good night."

"Good night."

"Good night." He smiled—and suddenly there seemed to be a pleasant significance in having been among the last to go, as if he had desired it all the time. "Good night, old sport. . . . Good night."

But as I walked down the steps I saw that the evening was not quite over.

Fifty feet from the door a dozen headlights illuminated a bizarre and tumultuous scene.

A man in a long duster dismounted from the wreck and now stood in the middle of the road, looking from the car to the tire and from the tire to the observers in a pleasant, puzzled way.

"See!" he explained. "It went in the ditch."

A man looking at the accident scene

The fact was infinitely astonishing to him—and I recognized first the unusual quality of wonder and then the man—it was the late patron of Gatsby's library.

"How'd it happen?"

He shrugged his shoulders.

"I know nothing whatever about mechanics," he said decisively.

"But how did it happen? Did you run into the wall?"

"Don't ask me," said Owl Eyes, washing his hands of the whole matter.

"I know very little about driving—next to nothing. It happened, and that's all I know."

"Well, if you're a poor driver you oughtn't to try driving at night."

"But I wasn't even trying," he explained indignantly, "I wasn't even trying."

An awed hush fell upon the bystanders.

I turned away and cut across the lawn toward home. I glanced back once. A wafer of a moon was shining over Gatsby's house, making the night fine as before and surviving the laughter and the sound of his still glowing garden. A sudden emptiness seemed to flow now from the windows and the great doors.

Reading over what I have written so far I see I have given the impression that the events of three nights several weeks apart were all that absorbed me. On the contrary they were merely casual events in a crowded summer and, until much later, they absorbed me infinitely less than my personal affairs.

Most of the time I worked. In the early morning the sun threw my shadow westward as I hurried down the white chasms of lower New York to the

Probity Trust. I knew the other clerks and young bond-salesmen by their first names and lunched with them in dark crowded restaurants on little pig sausages and mashed potatoes and coffee.

I even had a short affair with a girl who lived in Jersey City and worked in the accounting department, but her brother began throwing mean looks in my direction so when she went on her vacation in July I let it blow quietly away.

For a while I lost sight of Jordan Baker, and then in midsummer I found her again. At first I was flattered to go places with her because she was a golf champion and every one knew her name. Then it was something more. I wasn't actually in love, but I felt a sort of tender curiosity.

Chapter 4

On Sunday morning while church bells rang in the villages along shore the world and its mistress returned to Gatsby's house and twinkled hilariously on his lawn.

"He's a bootlegger," said the young ladies, moving somewhere between his cocktails and his flowers. "One time he killed a man who had found out that he was nephew to von Hindenburg and second cousin to the devil.

Reach me a rose, honey, and pour me a last drop into that there crystal glass."

At nine o'clock, one morning late in July Gatsby's gorgeous car lurched up the rocky drive to my door and gave out a burst of melody from its three noted horn. It was the first time he had called on me though I had gone to two of his parties, mounted in his hydroplane, and, at his urgent invitation, made frequent use of his beach.

"Good morning, old sport. You're having lunch with me today and I thought we'd ride up together."

I had talked with him perhaps half a dozen times in the past month and found, to my disappointment, that he had little to say.

So my first impression, that he was a person of some undefined consequence, gradually faded and

Gatsby's gorgeous car lurched up the rocky drive to Nick's door

he became simply the proprietor of an elaborate roadhouse next door.

And then came that disconcerting ride. We hadn't reached West Egg village before Gatsby began leaving his elegant sentences unfinished and slapping himself indecisively on the knee of his caramel-colored suit.

"Look here, old sport," he broke out surprisingly. "What's your opinion of me, anyhow?"

A little overwhelmed, I began the generalized evasions which that question deserves.

"Well, I'm going to tell you something about my life," he interrupted.

"I don't want you to get a wrong idea of me from all these stories you hear."

So he was aware of the bizarre accusations that flavored conversation in his halls.

"I am the son of some wealthy people in the middle-west—all dead now. I was brought up in America but educated at Oxford because all my ancestors have been educated there for many years. It is a family tradition."

"What part of the middle-west?" I inquired casually.

"San Francisco."

"I see."

"My family all died and I came into a good deal of money."

His voice was solemn as if the memory of that sudden extinction of a clan still haunted him. For a moment I suspected that he was pulling my leg but a glance at him convinced me otherwise.

"After that I lived like a young rajah in all the capitals of

Europe—Paris, Venice, Rome—collecting jewels, chiefly rubies, hunting big game, painting a little, things for myself only, and trying to forget something very sad that had happened to me long ago."

"Then came the war, old sport. It was a great relief and I tried very hard to die but I seemed to bear an enchanted life. I accepted a commission as first lieutenant when it began. In the Argonne Forest I took two machine-gun detachments so far forward that there was a half mile gap on either side of us where the infantry couldn't advance. We stayed there two days and two nights, a hundred and thirty men with sixteen Lewis guns, and when the infantry came up at last they found the insignia of three German divisions among the piles of dead. I was promoted to be a major and every Allied government gave me a decoration—even Montenegro, little Montenegro down on the Adriatic Sea!"

He reached in his pocket and a piece of metal, slung on a ribbon, fell into my palm.

"That's the one from Montenegro."

To my astonishment, the thing had an authentic look.

"I'm going to make a big request of you today," he said, "so I thought you ought to know something about me. I didn't want you to think I was just some nobody. You see, I usually find myself among strangers because I drift here and there trying to forget the sad thing that happened to me." He hesitated.

"You'll hear about it this afternoon."

"At lunch?"

"No, this afternoon. I happened to find out that you're taking Miss Baker to tea."

"Do you mean you're in love with Miss Baker?"

"No, old sport, I'm not. But Miss Baker has kindly consented to speak to you about this matter."

I hadn't the faintest idea what "this matter" was, but I was more annoyed than interested. I hadn't asked Jordan to tea in order to discuss Mr. Jay Gatsby. I was sure the request would be something utterly fantastic and for a moment I was sorry I'd ever set foot upon his overpopulated lawn.

He wouldn't say another word. His correctness grew on him as we neared the city. We passed Port Roosevelt.

With fenders spread like wings we scattered light through half Astoria—only half, for as we twisted among the pillars of the elevated I heard the familiar "jug—jug—SPAT!" of a motor cycle, and a frantic policeman rode alongside.

A piece of metal falls

"All right, old sport," called Gatsby. We slowed down. Taking a white card from his wallet he waved it before the man's eyes.

"Right you are," agreed the policeman, tipping his cap. "Know you next time, Mr. Gatsby. Excuse ME!"

"What was that?" I inquired. "The picture of Oxford?"

"I was able to do the commissioner a favor once, and he sends me a

Christmas card every year."

Over the great bridge, with the sunlight through the girders making a constant flicker upon the moving cars, with the city rising up across the river in white heaps and sugar lumps all built with a wish out of non-olfactory money. The city seen from the Queensboro Bridge is always the city seen for the first time, in its first wild promise of all the mystery and the beauty in the world.

Roaring noon. In a well-fanned Forty-second Street cellar I met Gatsby for lunch. Blinking away the brightness of the street outside my eyes picked him out obscurely in the anteroom, talking to another man.

"Mr. Carraway this is my friend Mr. Wolfshiem."

A small, flat-nosed Jew raised his large head and regarded me with two fine growths of hair which luxuriated in either nostril. After a moment I discovered his tiny eyes in the half darkness.

Gatsby took an arm of each of us and moved forward into the Restaurant.

"Look here, old sport," said Gatsby, leaning toward me, "I'm afraid I made you a little angry this morning in the car."

There was the smile again, but this time I held out against it.

"I don't like mysteries," I answered. "And I don't understand why you won't come out frankly and tell me what you want. Why has it all got to come through Miss Baker?"

"Oh, it's nothing underhand," he assured me. "Miss Baker's a great sportswoman, you know, and she'd never do anything that wasn't all right."

Suddenly he looked at his watch, jumped up and hurried from the room leaving me with Mr. Wolfshiem at the table.

After lunch, I insisted on paying the check. As the waiter brought my change I caught sight of Tom Buchanan across the crowded room.

"Come along with me for a minute," I said. "I've got to say hello to someone."

When he saw us Tom jumped up and took half a dozen steps in our direction.

"Where've you been?" he demanded eagerly. "Daisy's furious because you haven't called up."

"This is Mr. Gatsby, Mr. Buchanan."

They shook hands briefly and a strained, unfamiliar look of embarrassment came over Gatsby's face.

"How've you been, anyhow?" demanded Tom of me. "How'd you happen to come up this far to eat?"

"I've been having lunch with Mr. Gatsby."

I turned toward Mr. Gatsby, but he was no longer there.

One October day in 1917—— (said Jordan Baker that afternoon, sitting up very straight on a straight chair in the tea-garden at the Plaza Hotel) —I was walking along from one place to another half on the sidewalks and half on the lawns.

The largest of the lawns belonged to Daisy Fay's house. She was just eighteen, two years older than me, and by far the most popular of all the young girls in Louisville. She dressed in white, and had a little white roadster and all day long the telephone rang in her house.

When I came opposite her house that morning her white roadster was beside the curb, and she was sitting in it with a lieutenant I had never seen before. They were so engrossed in each other that she didn't see me until

I was five feet away.

"Hello Jordan," she called unexpectedly. "Please come here."

I was flattered that she wanted to speak to me, because of all the older girls I admired her most. She

Gatsby introduces Nick to Mr. Wolfshiem

asked me if I was going to the Red Cross and make bandages. I was. Well, then, would I tell them that she couldn't come that day? The officer looked at Daisy while she was speaking, in a way that every young girl wants to be looked at sometime, and because it seemed romantic to me I have remembered the incident ever since. His name was Jay Gatsby and I didn't lay eyes on him again for over four years—even after I'd met him on Long Island I didn't realize it was the same man.

That was 1917. By the next year I had a few beaux myself, and I began to play in tournaments, so I didn't see Daisy very often.

She went with a slightly older crowd—when she went with anyone at all.

Wild rumors were circulating about her—how her mother had found her packing her bag one winter night to go to New York and say goodbye to a soldier who was going overseas. She was effectually prevented, but she wasn't on speaking terms with her family for several weeks. After that she didn't play around with the soldiers any more but only with a few flat-footed, short-sighted young men in town who couldn't get into the army at all.

By the next autumn she was gay again, gay as ever. In June she married Tom Buchanan of Chicago with more pomp and circumstance than Louisville ever knew before. He came down with a hundred people in four private cars and hired a whole floor of the Seelbach Hotel. The day before the wedding he gave her a string of pearls valued at three hundred and fifty thousand dollars.

I was bridesmaid. I came into her room half an hour before the bridal dinner, and found her lying on her bed as lovely as the June night in her flowered dress—and as drunk as a monkey. She had a bottle of sauterne in one hand and a letter in the other.

" 'Gratulate me," she muttered. "Never had a drink before but oh, how I do enjoy it."

"What's the matter, Daisy?"

I was scared, I can tell you; I'd never seen a girl like that before.

"Here, dearies." She groped around in a wastebasket she had with her on the bed and pulled out the string of pearls. "Take 'em downstairs and give 'em back to whoever they belong to. Tell 'em all Daisy's change' her mine. Say 'Daisy's change' her mine!'."

She began to cry—she cried and cried. I rushed out and found her mother's maid and we locked the door and got her into a cold bath. She wouldn't let go of the letter. She took it into the tub with her and squeezed it up into a wet ball, and only let me leave it in the soap dish when she saw that it was coming to pieces like snow.

But she didn't say another word. We gave her spirits of ammonia and put ice on her forehead and hooked her back into her dress and half an hour later when we walked out of the room the pearls were around her neck and the incident was over. Next day at five o'clock she married Tom Buchanan without so much as a shiver and started off on a three months' trip to the South Seas.

I saw them in Santa Barbara when they came back and I thought I'd never seen a girl so mad about her husband. If he left the room for a minute she'd look around uneasily and say "Where's Tom gone?" and wear the most abstracted expression until she saw him coming in the door.

A week after I left Santa

Barbara Tom ran into a wagon on the Ventura road one night and ripped a front wheel off his car. The girl who was with him got into the papers too because her arm was broken—she was one of the chambermaids in the Santa Barbara Hotel.

The next April Daisy had her little girl and they went to France for a year.

Well, about six weeks ago, she heard the name Gatsby for the first time in years. It was when I asked you—do you remember?—if you knew Gatsby in West Egg. After you had gone home she came into my room and woke me up, and said "What Gatsby?" and when I described him—I was half asleep—she said in the strangest voice that it must be the man she used to know. It wasn't until then that I connected this Gatsby with the officer in her white car.

When Jordan Baker finished telling all this we had left the Plaza for half an hour and were driving in a Victoria through Central Park.

Jordan and Nick in conversation

"It was a strange coincidence," I said.

"But it wasn't a coincidence at all."

"Why not?"

"Gatsby bought that house so that Daisy would be just across the bay."

Then it had not been merely the stars to which he had aspired on that June night.

He came alive to me, delivered suddenly from the womb of his purposeless splendor.

"He wants to know—" continued Jordan "—if you'll invite Daisy to your house some afternoon and then let him come over."

The modesty of the demand shook me.

He waited five years and bought a mansion where he dispensed starlight to casual moths so that he could "come over" some afternoon to a stranger's garden.

"Did I have to know all this before he could ask such a little thing?"

"He's afraid. He's waited so long. He thought you might be offended. You see he's a regular tough underneath it all."

Something worried me.

"Why didn't he ask you to arrange a meeting?"

"He wants her to see his house," she explained.

"And your house is right next door."

"Oh!"

"I think he half expected her to wander into one of his parties, some night," went on Jordan, "but she never did. Then he began asking people casually if they knew her, and I was the first one he found.

It was that night he sent for me at his dance, and you should have heard the elaborate way he worked up to it. Of course, I immediately suggested a luncheon in New York—and I thought he'd go mad:

" 'I don't want to do anything out of the way!' he kept saying. 'I want to see her right next door.'

"When I said you were a particular friend of Tom's he started to abandon the whole idea. He doesn't know very much about Tom, though he says he's read a Chicago paper for years just on the chance of catching a glimpse of Daisy's name."

It was dark now, and as we dipped under a little bridge I put my arm around Jordan's golden shoulder and drew her toward me and asked her to dinner.

Suddenly I wasn't thinking of Daisy and Gatsby any more but of this clean, hard, limited person who dealt in universal skepticism and who leaned back jauntily just within the circle of my arm.

A phrase began to beat in my ears with a sort of heady excitement: "There are only the pursued, the pursuing, the busy and the tired."

"And Daisy ought to have something in her life," murmured Jordan to me.

Jordan and Nick on a bridge

"Does she want to see Gatsby?"

"She's not to know about it. Gatsby doesn't want her to know. You're just supposed to invite her to tea."

We passed a barrier of dark trees, and then the facade of Fifty-ninth

Street, a block of delicate pale light, beamed down into the park.

Unlike Gatsby and Tom Buchanan I had no girl whose disembodied face floated along the dark cornices and blinding signs and so I drew up the girl beside me, tightening my arms. Her wan, scornful mouth smiled and so

I drew her up again, closer, this time to my face.

Chapter 5

When I came home to West Egg that night I was afraid for a moment that my house was on fire. Two o'clock and the whole corner of the peninsula was blazing with light which fell unreal on the shrubbery and made thin elongating glints upon the roadside wires. Turning a corner I saw that it was Gatsby's house, lit from tower to cellar.

But there wasn't a sound. Only wind in the trees which blew the wires and made the lights go off and on again as if the house had winked into the darkness. As my taxi groaned away I saw Gatsby walking toward me across his lawn.

"Your place looks like the world's fair," I said.

"Does it?" He turned his eyes toward it absently. "I have been glancing into some of the rooms. Let's go to Coney Island, old sport. In my car."

"It's too late."

"Well, suppose we take a plunge in the swimming pool? I haven't made use of it all summer."

"I've got to go to bed."

"All right." He waited, looking at me with suppressed eagerness.

Nick looks at Gatsby

"I talked with Miss Baker," I said after a moment. "I'm going to call up Daisy tomorrow and invite her over here to tea."

"Oh, that's all right," he said carelessly. "I don't want to put you to any trouble."

"What day would suit you?"

"How about the day after tomorrow?" He considered for a moment. Then, with reluctance:

"I want to get the grass cut," he said.

"There's another little thing," he said uncertainly, and hesitated.

"Would you rather put it off for a few days?" I asked.

"Oh, it isn't about that. At least——" He fumbled with a series of beginnings. "Why, I thought—why, look here, old sport, you don't make much money, do you?"

"Not very much."

This seemed to reassure him and he continued more confidently.

"I thought you didn't, if you'll pardon my—you see, I carry on a little business on the side, a sort of sideline, you understand. And I thought that if you don't make very much—You're selling bonds, aren't you, old sport?"

"Trying to."

"Well, this would interest you. It wouldn't take up much of your time and you might pick up a nice bit of money. It happens to be a rather confidential sort of thing."

I realize now that under different circumstances that conversation might have been one of the crises of my life. But, because the offer was obviously and tactlessly for a service to be rendered, I had no choice except to cut him off there.

"I've got my hands full," I said. "I'm much obliged but I couldn't take on any more work."

"You wouldn't have to do any business with Wolfshiem." He waited a moment longer, hoping I'd begin a conversation, but I was too absorbed to be responsive, so he went unwillingly home.

The evening had made me light-headed and happy. I called up Daisy from the office next morning and invited her to come to tea.

"Don't bring Tom," I warned her.

The day agreed upon was pouring rain. At eleven o'clock a man in a raincoat dragging a lawn-mower tapped at my front door and said that

Mr. Gatsby had sent him over to cut my grass.

An hour later the front door opened nervously, and Gatsby in a white flannel suit, silver shirt and gold-colored tie hurried in. He was pale and there were dark signs of sleeplessness beneath his eyes.

"Is everything all right?" he asked immediately.

"The grass looks fine, if that's what you mean."

"What grass?" he inquired blankly. "Oh, the grass in the yard." He looked out the window at it, but judging from his expression I don't believe he saw a thing.

The rain cooled about half-past three to a damp mist through which occasional thin drops swam like dew. Gatsby looked with vacant eyes through a copy of Clay's "Economics." Finally he got up and informed me in an uncertain voice that he was going home.

"Why's that?"

"Nobody's coming to tea. It's too late!" He looked at his watch as if there was some pressing demand on his time elsewhere. "I can't wait all day."

"Don't be silly; it's just two minutes to four."

He sat down, miserably, as if I had pushed him, and simultaneously there was the sound of a motor turning into my lane. We both jumped up and, a little harrowed myself, I went out into the yard.

Under the dripping bare lilac trees a large open car was coming up the drive. It stopped. Daisy's face, tipped sideways beneath a three-cornered lavender hat, looked out at me with a bright ecstatic smile.

"Is this absolutely where you live, my dearest one?"

A damp streak of hair lay like a dash of blue paint across her cheek and her hand was wet with glistening drops as I took it to help her from the car.

Daisy comes to meet Gatsby

"Are you in love with me," she said low in my ear. "Or why did I have to come alone?"

"That's the secret of Castle Rackrent. Tell your chauffeur to go far away and spend an hour."

We went in. To my overwhelming surprise the living room was deserted.

"Well, that's funny!" I exclaimed.

"What's funny?"

She turned her head as there was a light, dignified knocking at the front door.

I went out and opened it. Gatsby, pale as death, with his hands plunged like weights in his coat pockets, was standing in a puddle of water glaring tragically into my eyes.

With his hands still in his coat pockets he stalked by me into the hall, turned sharply as if he were on a wire and disappeared into the living room.

It wasn't a bit funny. Aware of the loud beating of my own heart I pulled the door to against the increasing rain.

For half a minute there wasn't a sound. Then from the living room I heard a sort of choking murmur and part of a laugh followed by Daisy's voice on a clear artificial note.

"I certainly am awfully glad to see you again."

A pause; it endured horribly. I had nothing to do in the hall so I went into the room.

Gatsby, his hands still in his pockets, was reclining against the mantelpiece in a strained counterfeit of perfect ease, even of boredom.

His head leaned back so far that it rested against the face of a defunct mantelpiece clock and from this position his distraught eyes stared down at Daisy who was sitting frightened but graceful on the edge of a stiff chair.

"We've met before," muttered Gatsby. His eyes glanced momentarily at me and his lips parted with an abortive attempt at a laugh.

"I'm sorry about the clock," he said.

"It's an old clock," I told them idiotically.

"We haven't met for many years," said Daisy, her voice as matter-of-fact as it could ever be.

"Five years next November."

Gatsby got himself into a shadow and while Daisy and I talked looked conscientiously from one to the other of us with tense unhappy eyes.

However, as calmness wasn't an end in itself I made an excuse at the first possible moment and got to my feet.

"Where are you going?" demanded Gatsby in immediate alarm.

"I'll be back."

"I've got to speak to you about something before you go."

He followed me wildly into the kitchen, closed the door and whispered:

"Oh, God!" in a miserable way.

"What's the matter?"

"This is a terrible mistake," he said, shaking his head from side to side, "a terrible, terrible mistake."

"You're just embarrassed, that's all," and luckily I added: "Daisy's embarrassed too."

"She's embarrassed?" he repeated incredulously.

"Just as much as you are."

"Don't talk so loud."

"You're acting like a little boy," I broke out impatiently. "Not only that but you're rude. Daisy's sitting in there all alone."

He raised his hand to stop my words, looked at me with unforgettable reproach and opening the door cautiously went back into the other room.

I walked out the back way.

I went in—after making every possible noise in the kitchen short of pushing over the stove—but I don't believe they heard a sound.

They were sitting at either end of the couch looking at each other as if some question had been asked or was in the air, and every vestige of embarrassment was gone. Daisy's face was smeared with tears and when I came in she jumped up and began wiping at it with her handkerchief before a mirror.

Gatsby and Daisy looking at each other

But there was a change in Gatsby that was simply confounding.

He literally glowed; without a word or a gesture of exultation a new well-being radiated from him and filled the little room.

"Oh, hello, old sport," he said, as if he hadn't seen me for years. I thought for a moment he was going to shake hands.

"It's stopped raining."

"Has it?" When he realized what I was talking about, that there were twinkle-bells of sunshine in the room, he smiled like a weather man, like an ecstatic patron of recurrent light, and repeated the news to Daisy.

"What do you think of that? It's stopped raining."

"I'm glad, Jay." Her throat, full of aching, grieving beauty, told only of her unexpected joy.

"I want you and Daisy to come over to my house," he said, "I'd like to show her around."

"You're sure you want me to come?"

"Absolutely, old sport."

Daisy went upstairs to wash her face—too late I thought with humiliation of my towels—while Gatsby and I waited on the lawn.

"My house looks well, doesn't it?" he demanded. "See how the whole front of it catches the light."

"Yes." His eyes went over it, every arched door and square tower. "It took me just three years to earn the money that bought it."

"I thought you inherited your money."

"I did, old sport," he said automatically, "but I lost most of it in the big panic—the panic of the war."

I think he hardly knew what he was saying, for when I asked him what business he was in he answered "That's my affair," before he realized that it wasn't the appropriate reply.

"Oh, I've been in several things," he corrected himself. "I was in the drug business and then I was in the oil business. But I'm not in either one now." He looked at me with more attention. "Do you mean you've been thinking over what I proposed the other night?"

Before I could answer, Daisy came out of the house and two rows of brass buttons on her dress gleamed in the sunlight.

"That huge place THERE?" she cried pointing.

"Do you like it?"

"I love it, but I don't see how you live there all alone."

"I keep it always full of interesting people, night and day. People who do interesting things. Celebrated people."

Instead of taking the short cut along the Sound we went down the road and entered by the big postern.

And inside as we wandered through Marie Antoinette music rooms and Restoration salons I felt that there were guests concealed behind every couch and table, under orders to be breathlessly silent until we had passed through.

We went upstairs, through period bedrooms swathed in rose and lavender silk and vivid with new flowers, through dressing rooms and poolrooms, and bathrooms with sunken baths—intruding into one chamber where a dishevelled man in pajamas was doing liver exercises on the floor.

It was Mr. Klipspringer, the "boarder." I had seen him wandering hungrily about the beach that morning.

Finally we came to Gatsby's own apartment, a bedroom and a bath and an Adam study, where we sat down and drank a glass of some Chartreuse he took from a cupboard in the wall.

He hadn't once ceased looking at Daisy and I think he revalued everything in his house according to the measure of response it drew from her well-loved eyes.

His bedroom was the simplest room of all—except where the dresser was garnished with a toilet set of pure dull gold.

He opened for us two hulking patent cabinets which held his massed suits and dressing-gowns and ties, and his shirts, piled like bricks in stacks a dozen high.

Daisy and Gatsby in love

"I've got a man in England who buys me clothes. He sends over a selection of things at the beginning of each season, spring and fall."

After the house, we were to see the grounds and the swimming pool, and the hydroplane and the midsummer flowers—but outside Gatsby's window it began to rain again so we stood in a row looking at the corrugated surface of the Sound.

"If it wasn't for the mist we could see your home across the bay," said

Gatsby. "You always have a green light that burns all night at the end of your dock."

Daisy put her arm through his abruptly but he seemed absorbed in what he had just said. Possibly it occurred to him that the colossal significance of that light had now vanished forever.

Compared to the great distance that had separated him from Daisy it had seemed very near to her, almost touching her. It had seemed as close as a star to the moon. Now it was again a green light on a dock.

His count of enchanted objects had diminished by one.

The rain was still falling, but the darkness had parted in the west, and there was a pink and golden billow of foamy clouds above the sea.

"Look at that," she whispered, and then after a moment: "I'd like to just get one of those pink clouds and put you in it and push you around."

I tried to go then, but they wouldn't hear of it; perhaps my presence made them feel more satisfactorily alone.

"I know what we'll do," said Gatsby, "we'll have Klipspringer play the piano."

He went out of the room calling "Ewing!" and returned in a few minutes accompanied by an embarrassed, slightly worn young man with shell-rimmed glasses and scanty blonde hair. He was now decently clothed in a "sport shirt" open at the neck, sneakers and duck trousers of a nebulous hue.

In the music room Gatsby turned on a solitary lamp beside the piano. He lit Daisy's cigarette from a trembling match, and sat down with her on a couch far across the room where there was no light save what the gleaming floor bounced in from the hall.

When Klipspringer played "The Love Nest" he turned around on the bench and searched unhappily for Gatsby in the gloom.

Outside the wind was loud and there was a faint flow of thunder along the

Sound. All the lights were going on in West Egg now; the electric trains, men-carrying, were plunging home through the rain from New York. It was the hour of a profound human change, and excitement was generating on the air.

As I went over to say goodbye I saw that the expression of bewilderment had come back into

Gatsby's face, as though a faint doubt had occurred to him as to the quality of his present happiness. Almost five years!

As I watched him he adjusted himself a little, visibly. His hand took hold of hers and as she said something low in his ear he turned toward her with a rush of emotion. I think that voice held him most with its fluctuating, feverish warmth because it couldn't be over-dreamed—that voice was a deathless song.

They had forgotten me, but Daisy glanced up and held out her hand;

Gatsby didn't know me now at all. I looked once more at them and they looked back at me, remotely, possessed by intense life. Then I went out of the room and down the marble steps into the rain, leaving them there together.

Chapter 6

About this time an ambitious young reporter from New York arrived one morning at Gatsby's door and asked him if he had anything to say.

"Anything to say about what?" inquired Gatsby politely.

"Why,—any statement to give out."

It transpired after a confused five minutes that the man had heard

Gatsby's name around his office in a connection which he either wouldn't reveal or didn't fully understand.

It was a random shot, and yet the reporter's instinct was right. Gatsby's notoriety, spread about by the hundreds who had accepted his hospitality and so become authorities on his past, had increased all summer until he fell just short of being news. Just why these inventions were a source of satisfaction to James Gatz of North Dakota, isn't easy to say.

James Gatz—that was really, or at least legally, his name. He changed it at the age of seventeen and at the specific moment that witnessed the beginning of his career—when he saw Dan Cody's yacht drop anchor over the most insidious flat on Lake Superior. It was James Gatz who had been loafing along the

Reporter at Gatsby's door

beach that afternoon in a torn green jersey and a pair of canvas pants, but it was already Jay Gatsby who borrowed a row-boat, pulled out to the TUOLOMEE and informed Cody that a wind might catch him and break him up in half an hour.

His parents were shiftless and unsuccessful farm people—his imagination had never really accepted them as his parents at all. The truth was that

Jay Gatsby, of West Egg, Long Island, sprang from his Platonic conception of himself.

For over a year he had been beating his way along the south shore of

Lake Superior as a clam digger and a salmon fisher or in any other capacity that brought him food and bed.

His brown, hardening body lived naturally through the half fierce, half lazy work of the bracing days.

An instinct toward his future glory had led him, some months before, to the small Lutheran college of St. Olaf in southern Minnesota.

He stayed there two weeks. Then he drifted back to Lake Superior, and he was still searching for something to do on the day that Dan Cody's yacht dropped anchor in the shallows along shore.

Cody was fifty years old then, a product of the Nevada silver fields, of the Yukon, of every rush for metal since Seventy-five.

He had been coasting along all too hospitable shores for five years when he turned up as James Gatz's destiny at Little Girl Bay.

To the young Gatz, resting on his oars and looking up at the railed deck, the yacht represented all the beauty and glamour in the world. I suppose he smiled at Cody—he had probably discovered that people liked him when he smiled. At any rate Cody asked him a few questions (one of them elicited the brand new name) and found that he was quick, and extravagantly ambitious. A few days later he took him to Duluth and bought him a blue coat, six pair of white duck trousers and a yachting cap. And when the TUOLOMEE left for the West Indies and the Barbary

Coast Gatsby left too.

He was employed in a vague personal capacity— while he remained with

Cody he was in turn steward, mate, skipper, secretary, and even jailor.

The arrangement lasted five years during which the boat went three times around the continent. It might have lasted indefinitely except for the fact that Ella Kaye came on board one night in Boston and a week later Dan Cody inhospitably died.

And it was from Cody that he inherited money—a legacy of twenty-five thousand dollars. He didn't get it. He never understood the legal device that was used against him but what remained of the millions went

Nick at Gatsby's house and Tom comes in

intact to Ella Kaye. He was left with his singularly appropriate education; the vague contour of Jay Gatsby had filled out to the substantiality of a man.

He told me all this very much later, but I've put it down here with the idea of exploding those first wild rumors about his antecedents, which weren't even faintly true.

It was a halt, too, in my association with his affairs. For several weeks I didn't see him or hear his voice on the phone—mostly I was in New York, trotting around with Jordan and trying to ingratiate myself with her senile aunt. But finally I went over to his house one Sunday afternoon. I hadn't been there two minutes when somebody brought Tom Buchanan in for a drink. I was startled, naturally, but the really surprising thing was that it hadn't happened before.

They were a party of three on horseback—Tom and a man named Sloane and a pretty woman in a brown riding habit who had been there previously.

"I'm delighted to see you," said Gatsby standing on his porch.

"I'm delighted that you dropped in."

As though they cared!

"Sit right down. Have a cigarette or a cigar." He walked around the room quickly, ringing bells. "I'll have something to drink for you in just a minute."

He was profoundly affected by the fact that Tom was there. But he would be uneasy anyhow until he had given them something, realizing in a vague way that that was all they came for. Mr. Sloane wanted nothing "Did you have a nice ride?"

"Very good roads around here."

Moved by an irresistible impulse, Gatsby turned to Tom who had accepted the introduction as a stranger.

"I believe we've met somewhere before, Mr. Buchanan."

"Oh, yes," said Tom, gruffly polite but obviously not remembering.

"So we did. I remember very well."

"About two weeks ago."

"That's right. You were with Nick here."

"I know your wife," continued Gatsby, almost aggressively.

"That so?"

Tom turned to me.

"You live near here, Nick?"

"Next door."

"That so?"

Mr. Sloane didn't enter into the conversation but lounged back haughtily

in his chair. "Why don't you—why don't you stay for supper? I wouldn't be surprised if some other people dropped in from New York."

"You come to supper with ME," said the lady enthusiastically.

"Both of you."

This included me.

"I'm afraid I won't be able to," I said.

"Well, you come," she urged, concentrating on Gatsby.

"We won't be late if we start now," she insisted aloud.

"I haven't got a horse," said Gatsby. "I used to ride in the army but

I've never bought a horse. I'll have to follow you in my car. Excuse me for just a minute."

The rest of us walked out on the porch, where Sloane and the lady began an impassioned conversation aside.

"My God, I believe the man's coming," said Tom. "Doesn't he know she doesn't want him?"

"She says she does want him."

"She has a big dinner party and he won't know a soul there." He frowned.

"I wonder where in the devil he met Daisy. By God, I may be old-fashioned in my ideas, but women run around too much these days to suit me. They meet all kinds of crazy fish."

Suddenly Mr. Sloane and the lady walked down the steps and mounted their horses.

All ready to go for a party

"Come on," said Mr. Sloane to Tom, "we're late. We've got to go." And then to me: "Tell him we couldn't wait, will you?"

Tom and I shook hands, the rest of us exchanged a cool nod and they trotted quickly down the drive, disappearing under the August foliage just as Gatsby with hat and light overcoat in hand came out the front door.

Tom was evidently perturbed at Daisy's running around alone, for on the following Saturday night he came with her to Gatsby's party. Perhaps his presence gave the evening its peculiar quality of oppressiveness.

They arrived at twilight and as we strolled out among the sparkling hundreds Daisy's voice was playing murmurous tricks in her throat.

"These things excite me SO," she whispered. "If you want to kiss me any time during the evening, Nick, just let me know and I'll be glad to arrange it for you. Just mention my name. Or present a green card.

I'm giving out green— —"

"Look around," suggested Gatsby.

"I'm looking around. I'm having a marvelous— —"

"You must see the faces of many people you've heard about."

Tom's arrogant eyes roamed the crowd.

"We don't go around very much," he said. "In fact I was just thinking

I don't know a soul here."

"Perhaps you know that lady." Gatsby indicated a gorgeous, scarcely human orchid of a woman who sat in state under a white plum tree. Tom and Daisy stared, with that peculiarly unreal feeling that accompanies the recognition of a hitherto ghostly celebrity of the movies.

"She's lovely," said Daisy.

"The man bending over her is her director."

He took them ceremoniously from group to group:

Daisy and Gatsby danced. I remember being surprised by his graceful, conservative fox-trot—I had never seen him dance before. Then they sauntered over to my house and sat on the steps for half an hour while at her request I remained watchfully in the garden: "In case there's a fire or a flood," she explained, "or any act of God."

Tom appeared from his oblivion as we were sitting down to supper together. "Do you mind if I eat with some people over here?" he said. "A fellow's getting off some funny stuff."

"Go ahead," answered Daisy genially.

After the party, I sat on the front steps with them while they waited for their car. It was dark here in front: only the bright door sent ten square feet of light volleying out into the soft black morning.

"Who is this Gatsby anyhow?" demanded Tom suddenly. "Some big bootlegger?"

"Where'd you hear that?" I inquired.

"I didn't hear it. I imagined it. A lot of these newly rich people are just big bootleggers, you know."

"Not Gatsby," I said shortly.

He was silent for a moment. The pebbles of the drive crunched under his feet.

"Well, he certainly must have strained himself to get this menagerie together."

A breeze stirred the grey haze of Daisy's fur collar.

"At least they're more interesting than the people we know," she said with an effort.

"You didn't look so interested."

"Well, I was."

Tom laughed and turned to me.

"I'd like to know who he is and what he does," insisted Tom. "And I think

I'll make a point of finding out."

"I can tell you right now," she answered. "He owned some drug stores,

a lot of drug stores. He built them up himself."

The dilatory limousine came rolling up the drive.

"Good night, Nick," said Daisy.

I stayed late that night. Gatsby asked me to wait until he was free and I lingered in the garden. When

Daisy and Gatsby dance

he came down the steps at last the tanned skin was drawn unusually tight on his face, and his eyes were bright and tired.

"She didn't like it," he said immediately.

"Of course she did."

"She didn't like it," he insisted. "She didn't have a good time." He was silent and I guessed at his unutterable depression.

"I feel far away from her," he said. "It's hard to make her understand."

He wanted nothing less of Daisy than that she should go to Tom and say:

"I never loved you." After she had obliterated three years with that sentence they could decide upon the more practical measures to be taken.

One of them was that, after she was free, they were to go back to

Louisville and be married from her house—just as if it were five years ago.

"And she doesn't understand," he said. "She used to be able to understand. We'd sit for hours——"

He broke off and began to walk up and down a desolate path of fruit rinds and discarded favors and crushed flowers.

"I wouldn't ask too much of her," I ventured. "You can't repeat the past."

"Can't repeat the past?" he cried incredulously. "Why of course you can!"

He looked around him wildly, as if the past were lurking here in the shadow of his house, just out of reach of his hand.

"I'm going to fix everything just the way it was before," he said, nodding determinedly. "She'll see."

He talked a lot about the past and I gathered that he wanted to recover something, some idea of himself perhaps, that had gone into loving Daisy.

Through all he said, even through his appalling sentimentality, I was reminded of something—an elusive rhythm, a fragment of lost words, that I had heard somewhere a long time ago.

Chapter 7

It was when curiosity about Gatsby was at its highest that the lights in his house failed to go on one Saturday night.

Wondering if he were sick I went over to find out — an unfamiliar butler with a villainous face squinted at me suspiciously from the door.

"Is Mr. Gatsby sick?"

"Nope."

"I hadn't seen him around, and I was rather worried. Tell him Mr. Carraway came over."

"Who?" he demanded rudely.

"Carraway."

"Carraway. All right, I'll tell him." Abruptly he slammed the door.

My Finn informed me that Gatsby dismissed every servant in his house a week ago and replaced them with half a dozen others, who never went into West Egg Village to be bribed by the tradesmen, but ordered moderate supplies over the telephone.

Next day Gatsby called me on the phone.

"Going away?" I inquired.

"No, old sport."

"I hear you fired all your servants."

A nurse with a girl enters the room

"I wanted somebody who wouldn't gossip. Daisy comes over quite often—in the afternoons."

So the whole caravansary had fallen in like a card house at the disapproval in her eyes.

"They're some people Wolfshiem wanted to do something for. They're all brothers and sisters. They used to run a small hotel."

"I see."

He was calling up at Daisy's request—would I come to lunch at her house tomorrow? Miss Baker would be there. Half an hour later

Daisy herself telephoned and seemed relieved to find that I was coming.

Something was up.

The next day was broiling, almost the last, certainly the warmest, of the summer. I took the train to East Egg for lunch at the house of Tom and Daisy. When I reached there, I found Gatsby and Jordan Baker there as well.

Gatsby stood in the center of the crimson carpet and gazed around with fascinated eyes. Daisy watched him and laughed, her sweet, exciting laugh; a tiny gust of powder rose from her bosom into the air.

Suddenly a freshly laundered nurse leading a little girl came into the room.

"Bles-sed pre-cious," she crooned, holding out her arms. "Come to your own mother that loves you."

The child, relinquished by the nurse, rushed across the room and rooted shyly into her mother's dress.

Gatsby and I in turn leaned down and took the small reluctant hand.

Afterward he kept looking at the child with surprise. I don't think he had ever really believed in its existence before.

"I got dressed before luncheon," said the child, turning eagerly to Daisy.

"That's because your mother wanted to show you off." Her face bent into the single wrinkle of the small white neck. "You dream, you. You absolute little dream."

"Yes," admitted the child calmly. "Aunt Jordan's got on a white dress too."

"How do you like mother's friends?" Daisy turned her around so that she faced Gatsby. "Do you think they're pretty?"

"Where's Daddy?"

"She doesn't look like her father," explained Daisy. "She looks like me.

She's got my hair and shape of the face."

Daisy sat back upon the couch. The nurse took a step forward and held out her hand.

"Come, Pammy."

"Goodbye, sweetheart!"

With a reluctant backward glance the well-disciplined child held to her nurse's hand and was pulled out the door, just as Tom came back, preceding four gin rickeys that clicked full of ice.

Gatsby took up his drink.

"I read somewhere that the sun's getting hotter every year," said Tom genially.

"It seems that pretty soon the earth's going to fall into the sun—or wait a minute—it's just the opposite—the sun's getting colder every year.

"Come outside," he suggested to Gatsby, "I'd like you to have a look at the place."

I went with them out to the veranda.

We had luncheon in the dining-room, darkened, too, against the heat, and drank down nervous gayety with the cold ale.

"What'll we do with ourselves this afternoon," cried Daisy, "and the day after that, and the next thirty years?"

"Don't be morbid," Jordan said. "Life starts all over again when it gets crisp in the fall."

"But it's so hot," insisted Daisy, on the verge of tears, "And everything's so confused. Let's all go to town!"

Her voice struggled on through the heat.

"Who wants to go to town?" demanded Daisy insistently. Gatsby's eyes floated toward her. "Ah," she cried, "you look so cool."

Daisy with her daughter

Their eyes met, and they stared together at each other, alone in space.

With an effort she glanced down at the table.

"You always look so cool," she repeated.

"All right," broke in Tom quickly, "I'm perfectly willing to go to town. Come on—we're all going to town."

He got up, his eyes still flashing between Gatsby and his wife.

No one moved.

They went upstairs to get ready while we three men stood there shuffling the hot pebbles with our feet. A silver curve of the moon hovered already in the western sky. Gatsby started to speak, changed his mind, but not before Tom wheeled and faced him expectantly.

"Have you got your stables here?" asked Gatsby with an effort.

"About a quarter of a mile down the road."

"Oh."

A pause.

"I don't see the idea of going to town," broke out Tom savagely.

"Women get these notions in their heads——"

"Shall we take anything to drink?" called Daisy from an upper window.

"I'll get some whiskey," answered Tom. He went inside.

Gatsby turned to me rigidly:

Tom came out of the house wrapping a quart bottle in a towel, followed by Daisy and Jordan wearing small tight hats of metallic cloth and carrying light capes over their arms.

"Shall we all go in my car?" suggested Gatsby.

"Come on, Daisy," said Tom, pressing her with his hand toward Gatsby's car. "I'll take you in this circus wagon."

He opened the door but she moved out from the circle of his arm.

"You take Nick and Jordan. We'll follow you in the coupé."

She walked close to Gatsby, touching his coat with her hand. Jordan and

Tom and I got into the front seat of Gatsby's car, Tom pushed the unfamiliar gears tentatively and we shot off into the oppressive heat leaving them out of sight behind.

Tom threw on both brakes impatiently and we slid to an abrupt dusty stop under Wilson's sign. After a moment the proprietor emerged from the interior of his establishment and gazed hollow-eyed at the car.

"Let's have some gas!" cried Tom roughly.

"I'm sick," said Wilson without moving. "I been sick all day."

"What's the matter?"

"I'm all run down."

"Well, shall I help myself?" Tom demanded.

"I didn't mean to interrupt your lunch," he said. "But I need money pretty bad."

"What do you want money for, all of a sudden?"

"I've been here too long. I want to get away. My wife and I want to go west."

"Your wife does!" exclaimed Tom, startled.

"She's been talking about it for ten years." He rested for a moment against the pump, shading his eyes. "And now she's going whether she wants to or not. I'm going to get her away."

The coupé flashed by us with a flurry of dust and the flash of a waving hand.

"What do I owe you?" demanded Tom harshly.

"I just got wised up to something funny the last two days," remarked

Wilson.

Wilson tells them that he has come to know that his wife is having an affair; he does not yet, however, know who her lover is.

In one of the windows over the garage the curtains had been moved aside a little and Myrtle Wilson was peering down at the car. So engrossed was she that she had no consciousness of being observed and one

Tom came out of the house wrapping a quart bottle, followed by Daisy and Jordan

emotion after another crept into her face like objects into a slowly developing picture.

Her expression was curiously familiar—it was an expression I had often seen on women's faces but on Myrtle Wilson's face it seemed purposeless and inexplicable until I realized that her eyes, wide with jealous terror, were fixed not on Tom, but on Jordan Baker, whom she took to be his wife.

There is no confusion like the confusion of a simple mind, and as we drove away Tom was feeling the hot whips of panic.

His wife and his mistress, until an hour ago secure and inviolate, were slipping precipitately from his control.

To escape from the summer heat, the group takes a suite at the Plaza Hotel.

The room was large and stifling, and, though it was already four o'clock, opening the windows admitted only a gust of hot shrubbery from the Park.

Daisy went to the mirror and stood with her back to us, fixing her hair.

"It's a swell suite," whispered Jordan respectfully and every one laughed.

"Open another window," commanded Daisy, without turning around.

"There aren't any more."

"Well, we'd better telephone for an axe——"

There was a moment of silence.

Tom now confronts Gatsby, mocking his use of the phrase "old sport."

"That was his cousin. I knew his whole family history before he left.

He gave me an aluminum putter that I use today."

"I want to ask Mr. Gatsby one more

Question," snapped Tom.

"Go on," Gatsby said politely.

"What kind of a row are you trying to cause in my house anyhow?"

They were out in the open at last and Gatsby was content.

"He isn't causing a row." Daisy looked desperately from one to the other. "You're causing a row. Please have a little self control."

"Self control!" repeated Tom incredulously.

"I suppose the latest thing is to sit back and let Mr. Nobody from Nowhere make love to your wife."

"I've got something to tell YOU, old sport,——" began Gatsby. But Daisy guessed at his intention.

"Please don't!" she interrupted helplessly. "Please let's all go home.

Why don't we all go home?"

"That's a good idea." I got up. "Come on, Tom. Nobody wants a drink."

"I want to know what Mr. Gatsby has to tell me."

"Your wife doesn't love you," said Gatsby. "She's never loved you.

She loves me."

"You must be crazy!" exclaimed Tom automatically.

Gatsby sprang to his feet, vivid with excitement.

"She never loved you, do you hear?" he cried.

"She only married you because I was poor and she was tired of waiting for me. It was a terrible mistake, but in her heart she never loved any one except me!"

At this point Jordan and I tried to go but Tom and Gatsby insisted with competitive firmness that we remain.

"Sit down Daisy." Tom's voice groped unsuccessfully for the paternal note.

"What's been going on? I want to hear all about it."

"I told you what's been going on," said Gatsby. "Going on for five years—and you didn't know."

Tom turned to Daisy sharply.

"You've been seeing this fellow for five years?"

"Not seeing," said Gatsby. "No, we couldn't meet. But both of us loved each other all that time, old sport, and you didn't know."

"Oh—that's all." Tom tapped his thick fingers together like a clergyman and leaned back in his chair.

Myrtle on the window over the garage looking at Tom, Nick and Jordan

"You're crazy!" he exploded.

"I can't speak about what happened five years ago, because I didn't know Daisy then—and I'll be damned if I see how you got within a mile of her unless you brought the groceries to the back door. But all the rest of that's a God Damned lie. Daisy loved me when she married me and she loves me now."

"No," said Gatsby, shaking his head.

"She does, though. The trouble is that sometimes she gets foolish ideas in her head and doesn't know what she's doing." He nodded sagely.

"And what's more, I love Daisy too. Once in a while I go off on a spree and make a fool of myself, but I always come back, and in my heart I love her all the time."

"You're revolting," said Daisy. She turned to me, and her voice, dropping an octave lower, filled the room with thrilling scorn: "Do you know why we left Chicago? I'm surprised that they didn't treat you to the story of that little spree."

Gatsby walked over and stood beside her.

"Daisy, that's all over now," he said earnestly. "It doesn't matter any more. Just tell him the truth—that you never loved him—and it's all wiped out forever."

She looked at him blindly. "Why,—how could I love him—possibly?"

"You never loved him."

She hesitated. Her eyes fell on Jordan and me with a sort of appeal, as though she realized at last what she was doing—and as though she had never, all along, intended doing anything at all. But it was done now.

It was too late.

"I never loved him," she said, with perceptible reluctance.

"Not at Kapiolani?" demanded Tom suddenly.

"No."

From the ballroom beneath, muffled and suffocating chords were drifting up on hot waves of air.

"Please don't." Her voice was cold, but the rancour was gone from it.

She looked at Gatsby. "There, Jay," she said—but her hand as she tried to light a cigarette was trembling. Suddenly she threw the cigarette and the burning match on the carpet.

"Oh, you want too much!" she cried to Gatsby. "I love you now—isn't that enough? I can't help what's past." She began to sob helplessly. "I did love him once—but I loved you too."

Gatsby's eyes opened and closed.

"You loved me TOO?" he repeated.

"Even that's a lie," said Tom savagely. "She didn't know you were alive.

Why,—there're things between Daisy and me that you'll never know, things that neither of us can ever forget."

The words seemed to bite physically into Gatsby.

"I want to speak to Daisy alone," he insisted. "She's all excited now——"

"Even alone I can't say I never loved Tom," she admitted in a pitiful voice. "It wouldn't be true."

"Of course it wouldn't," agreed Tom.

She turned to her husband.

"As if it mattered to you," she said.

"Of course it matters. I'm going to take better care of you from now on."

"You don't understand," said Gatsby, with a touch of panic. "You're not going to take care of her any more."

"I'm not?" Tom opened his eyes wide and laughed. He could afford to control himself now. "Why's that?"

"Daisy's leaving you."

"Nonsense."

"I am, though," she said with a visible effort.

"She's not leaving me!" Tom's words suddenly leaned down over Gatsby.

"I won't stand this!" cried Daisy. "Oh, please let's get out."

Nick and Gatsby in conversation with Daisy

I glanced at Daisy who was staring terrified between Gatsby and her husband and at Jordan who had begun to balance an invisible but absorbing object on the tip of her chin.

Then I turned back to Gatsby—and was startled at his expression. He looked—as if he had "killed a man."

Her frightened eyes told that whatever intentions, whatever courage she had had, were definitely gone.

"You two start on home, Daisy," said Tom. "In Mr. Gatsby's car."

She looked at Tom, alarmed now, but he insisted with magnanimous scorn.

"Go on. He won't annoy you. I think he realizes that his presumptuous little flirtation is over."

They were gone, without a word, snapped out, made accidental, isolated, like ghosts even from our pity.

After a moment Tom got up and began wrapping the unopened bottle of whiskey in the towel.

"Want any of this stuff? Jordan? . . . Nick?"

I didn't answer.

"Nick?" He asked again.

"What?"

"Want any?"

"No . . . I just remembered that today's my birthday."

I was thirty. Before me stretched the portentous menacing road of a new decade.

It was seven o'clock when we got into the coupé with him and started for Long Island.

Driving back, we witnessed a frightening scene on the border of the valley of ashes. Someone was hit by an automobile.

Michaelis, a Greek man who runs the restaurant next to Wilson's garage, was the witness. He told us that a car coming from New York City struck Myrtle and then sped away.

I realized that she must have been hit by Gatsby and Daisy, driving back from the city in Gatsby's big yellow automobile. Tom assumes that Gatsby was the driver.

After a while, we went back to Tom's house. Then I walked slowly down the drive away from the house intending to wait by the gate.

I hadn't gone twenty yards when I heard my name and Gatsby stepped from between two bushes into the path.

I must have felt pretty weird by that time because I could think of nothing except the luminosity of his pink suit under the moon.

"What are you doing?" I inquired.

"Just standing here, old sport."

Somehow, that seemed a despicable occupation. For all I knew he was going to rob the house in a moment; I wouldn't have been surprised to see sinister faces, the faces of "Wolfshiem's people," behind him in the dark shrubbery.

"Did you see any trouble on the road?" he asked after a minute.

"Yes."

He hesitated.

"Was she killed?"

"Yes."

"I thought so; I told Daisy I thought so. It's better that the shock should all come at once. She stood it pretty well."

He spoke as if Daisy's reaction was the only thing that mattered.

"I got to West Egg by a side road," he went on, "and left the car in my garage. I don't think anybody saw us but of course I can't be sure."

I disliked him so much by this time that I didn't find it necessary to tell him he was wrong.

"Who was the woman?" he inquired.

"Her name was Wilson. Her husband owns the garage. How the devil did it happen?"

"Well, I tried to swing the wheel— —" He broke off, and suddenly I guessed at the truth.

"Was Daisy driving?"

Michaelis tells them that a car struck Myrtle and sped away

"Yes," he said after a moment, "but of course I'll say I was. You see, when we left New York she was very nervous and she thought it would steady her to drive—and this woman rushed out at us just as we were passing a car coming the other way. It all happened in a minute but it seemed to me that she wanted to speak to us, thought we were somebody she knew. Well, first Daisy turned away from the woman toward the other car, and then she lost her nerve and turned back. The second my hand reached the wheel I felt the shock—it must have killed her instantly."

"It ripped her open— —"

"Don't tell me, old sport." He winced. "Anyhow—Daisy stepped on it.

I tried to make her stop, but she couldn't so I pulled on the emergency brake. Then she fell over into my lap and I drove on.

"She'll be all right tomorrow," he said presently. "I'm just going to wait here and see if he tries to bother her about that unpleasantness this afternoon. She's locked herself into her room and if he tries any brutality she's going to turn the light out and on again."

"He won't touch her," I said. "He's not thinking about her."

"I don't trust him, old sport."

"How long are you going to wait?"

"All night if necessary. Anyhow till they all go to bed."

A new point of view occurred to me. Suppose Tom found out that Daisy had been driving. He might think he saw a connection in it—he might think anything. I looked at the house: there were two or three bright windows downstairs and the pink glow from Daisy's room on the second floor.

"You wait here," I said. "I'll see if there's any sign of a commotion."

I walked back along the border of the lawn, traversed the gravel softly and tiptoed up the veranda steps. The drawing-room curtains were open, and I saw that the room was empty. Crossing the porch where we had dined that June night three months before I came to a small rectangle of light which I guessed was the pantry window. The blind was drawn but I found a rift at the sill.

Daisy and Tom were sitting opposite each other at the kitchen table with a plate of cold fried chicken between them and two bottles of ale. He was talking intently across the table at her and in his earnestness his hand had fallen upon and covered her own. Once in a while she looked up at him and nodded in agreement.

They weren't happy, and neither of them had touched the chicken or the ale—and yet they weren't unhappy either.

As I tiptoed from the porch I heard my taxi feeling its way along the dark road toward the house. Gatsby was waiting where I had left him in the drive.

"Is it all quiet up there?" he asked anxiously.

"Yes, it's all quiet." I hesitated. "You'd better come home and get some sleep."

He shook his head.

"I want to wait here till Daisy goes to bed. Good night, old sport."

He put his hands in his coat pockets and turned back eagerly to his scrutiny of the house, as though my presence marred the sacredness of the vigil. So I walked away and left him standing there in the moonlight—watching over nothing.

Chapter 8

I couldn't sleep all night; a fog-horn was groaning incessantly on the

Sound, and I tossed half-sick between grotesque reality and savage frightening dreams. Towards dawn I heard a taxi go up Gatsby's drive and immediately I jumped out of bed and began to dress—I felt that I had something to tell him, something to warn him about and morning would be too late.

Crossing his lawn I saw that his front door was still open and he was leaning against a table in the hall, heavy with dejection or sleep.

"Nothing happened," he said wanly. "I waited, and about four o'clock she came to the window and stood there for a minute and then turned out the light."

His house had never seemed so enormous to me as it did that night when we hunted through the great rooms for cigarettes.

We pushed aside curtains that were like pavilions and felt over innumerable feet of dark wall for electric light switches—once I tumbled with a sort of splash upon the keys of a ghostly piano.

There was an inexplicable amount of dust everywhere and the rooms were musty as though they hadn't been aired for many days.

Nick looks at Gatsby

Throwing open the French windows of the drawing-room we sat smoking out into the darkness.

"You ought to go away," I said. "It's pretty certain they'll trace your car."

"Go away NOW, old sport?"

"Go to Atlantic City for a week, or up to Montreal."

He wouldn't consider it. He couldn't possibly leave Daisy until he knew what she was going to do. He was clutching at some last hope and I couldn't bear to shake him free.

It was this night that he told me the strange story of his youth with Dan Cody—told it to me because "Jay Gatsby" had broken up like glass against Tom's hard malice and the long secret extravaganza was played out. I think that he would have acknowledged anything, now, without reserve, but he wanted to talk about Daisy.

She was the first "nice" girl he had ever known. In various unrevealed capacities he had come in contact with such people but always with indiscernible barbed wire between.

He found her excitingly desirable. He went to her house, at first with other officers from Camp Taylor, then alone. It amazed him—he had never been in such a beautiful house before.

But what gave it an air of breathless intensity was that Daisy lived there—it was as casual a thing to her as his tent out at camp was to him. There was a ripe mystery about it, a hint of bedrooms upstairs more beautiful and cool than other bedrooms, of gay and radiant activities taking place through its corridors and of romances that were not musty and laid away already in lavender.

It excited him too that many men already loved Daisy—it increased her value in his eyes. He felt their presence all about the house, pervading the air with the shades and echoes of still vibrant emotions.

But he knew that he was in Daisy's house by a colossal accident.

However glorious might be his future as Jay Gatsby, he was at present a penniless young man without a past, and at any moment the invisible cloak of his uniform might slip from his shoulders. So he made the most of his time.

He took what he could get, ravenously and unscrupulously—eventually he took Daisy one still October night, took her because he had no real right to touch her hand.

He might have despised himself, for he had certainly taken her under false pretenses. I don't mean that he traded on his phantom millions, but he had deliberately given Daisy a sense of security.

He let her believe that he was a person from much the same stratum as herself—that he was fully able to take care of her. As a matter of fact he had no such facilities.

Gatsby and Daisy

He had no comfortable family standing behind him and he was liable at the whim of an impersonal government to be blown anywhere about the world.

But he didn't despise himself and it didn't turn out as he imagined. He intended, probably, to take what he could and go—but now he found that he committed himself to the following of a grail.

He knew that Daisy was extraordinary but he didn't realize just how extraordinary a "nice" girl could be.

She vanished into her rich house, into her rich, full life, leaving Gatsby—nothing. He felt married to her, that was all.

When they met again two days later it was Gatsby who was breathless, who was somehow betrayed.

"I can't describe to you how surprised I was to find out I loved her, old sport. I even hoped for a while that she'd throw me over, but she didn't, because she was in love with me too. She thought I knew a lot because I knew different things from her. . . . Well, there I was, way off my ambitions, getting deeper in love every minute, and all of a sudden I didn't care. What was the use of doing great things if I could have a better time telling her what I was going to do?"

On the last afternoon before he went abroad he sat with Daisy in his arms for a long, silent time. It was a cold fall day with fire in the room and her cheeks flushed.

Now and then she moved and he changed his arm a little and once he kissed her dark shining hair. The afternoon made them tranquil for a while as if to give them a deep memory for the long parting the next day promised.

They had never been closer in their month of love nor communicated more profoundly one with another than when she brushed silent lips against his coat's shoulder or when he touched the end of her fingers, gently, as though she were asleep.

He did extraordinarily well in the war. He was a captain before he went to the front and following the Argonne battles he got his majority and the command of the divisional machine guns.

After the Armistice he tried frantically to get home but some complication or misunderstanding sent him to Oxford instead.

He was worried now—there was a quality of nervous despair in Daisy's letters. She didn't see why he couldn't come.

She was feeling the pressure of the world outside and she wanted to see him and feel his presence beside her and be reassured that she was doing the right thing after all.

For Daisy was young and her artificial world was redolent of orchids and pleasant, cheerful snobbery and orchestras which set the rhythm of the year, summing up the sadness and suggestiveness of life in new tunes.

All night the saxophones wailed the hopeless comment of the "Beale Street Blues" while a hundred pairs of golden and silver slippers shuffled the shining dust.

At the grey tea hour there were always rooms that throbbed incessantly with this low sweet fever, while fresh faces drifted here and there like rose petals blown by the sad horns around the floor.

Through this twilight universe Daisy began to move again with the season; suddenly she was again keeping half a dozen dates a day with half a dozen men and drowsing asleep at dawn with the beads and chiffon of an evening dress tangled among dying orchids on the floor beside her bed.

And all the time something within her was crying for a decision. She wanted her life shaped now, immediately—and the decision must be made by some force—of love, of money, of unquestionable practicality—that was close at hand.

That force took shape in the middle of spring with the arrival of Tom Buchanan.

There was a wholesome bulkiness about his person and his position and Daisy was flattered. Doubtless there was a certain struggle and a certain relief.

The letter reached Gatsby while he was still at Oxford.

It was dawn now on Long Island and we went about opening the rest of the windows downstairs, filling the house with grey turning, gold turning light.

Nick comes to meet Gatsby

The shadow of a tree fell abruptly across the dew and ghostly birds began to sing among the blue leaves.

There was a slow pleasant movement in the air, scarcely a wind, promising a cool lovely day.

"I don't think she ever loved him." Gatsby turned around from a window and looked at me challengingly.

"You must remember, old sport, she was very excited this afternoon. He told her those things in a way that frightened her—that made it look as if I was some kind of cheap sharper.

And the result was she hardly knew what she was saying."

He sat down gloomily.

"Of course she might have loved him, just for a minute, when they were first married—and loved me more even then, do you see?"

Suddenly he came out with a curious remark:

"In any case," he said, "it was just personal."

What could you make of that, except to suspect some intensity in his conception of the affair that couldn't be measured?

He came back from France when Tom and Daisy were still on their wedding trip, and made a miserable but irresistible journey to Louisville on the last of his army pay.

He stayed there a week, walking the streets where their footsteps had clicked together through the November night and revisiting the out-of-the-way places to which they had driven in her white car.

Just as Daisy's house had always seemed to him more mysterious and gay than other houses so his idea of the city itself, even though she was gone from it, was pervaded with a melancholy beauty.

It was nine o'clock when we finished breakfast and went out on the porch. The night had made a sharp difference in the weather and there was an autumn flavor in the air.

The gardener, the last one of Gatsby's former servants, came to the foot of the steps.

"I'm going to drain the pool today, Mr. Gatsby. Leaves will start falling pretty soon and then there's always trouble with the pipes."

"Don't do it today," Gatsby answered. He turned to me apologetically.

"You know, old sport, I've never used that pool all summer?"

I looked at my watch and stood up.

"Twelve minutes to my train."

I didn't want to go to the city. I wasn't worth a decent stroke of work but it was more than that—I didn't want to leave Gatsby.

I missed that train, and then another, before I could get myself away.

"I'll call you up," I said finally.

"Do, old sport."

"I'll call you about noon."

We walked slowly down the steps.

"I suppose Daisy'll call too." He looked at me anxiously as if he hoped I'd corroborate this.

"I suppose so."

"Well—goodbye."

We shook hands and I started away. Just before I reached the hedge I remembered something and turned around.

"They're a rotten crowd," I shouted across the lawn. "You're worth the whole damn bunch put together."

I've always been glad I said that. It was the only compliment I ever gave him, because I disapproved of him from beginning to end.

I thanked him for his hospitality. We were always thanking him for that—I and the others.

"Goodbye," I called. "I enjoyed breakfast, Gatsby."

Up in the city I tried for a while to list the quotations on an interminable amount of stock, then I fell asleep in my swivel-chair.

Just before noon the phone woke me and I started up with sweat breaking out on my forehead.

It was Jordan Baker; she often called me up at this hour because the uncertainty of her own movements

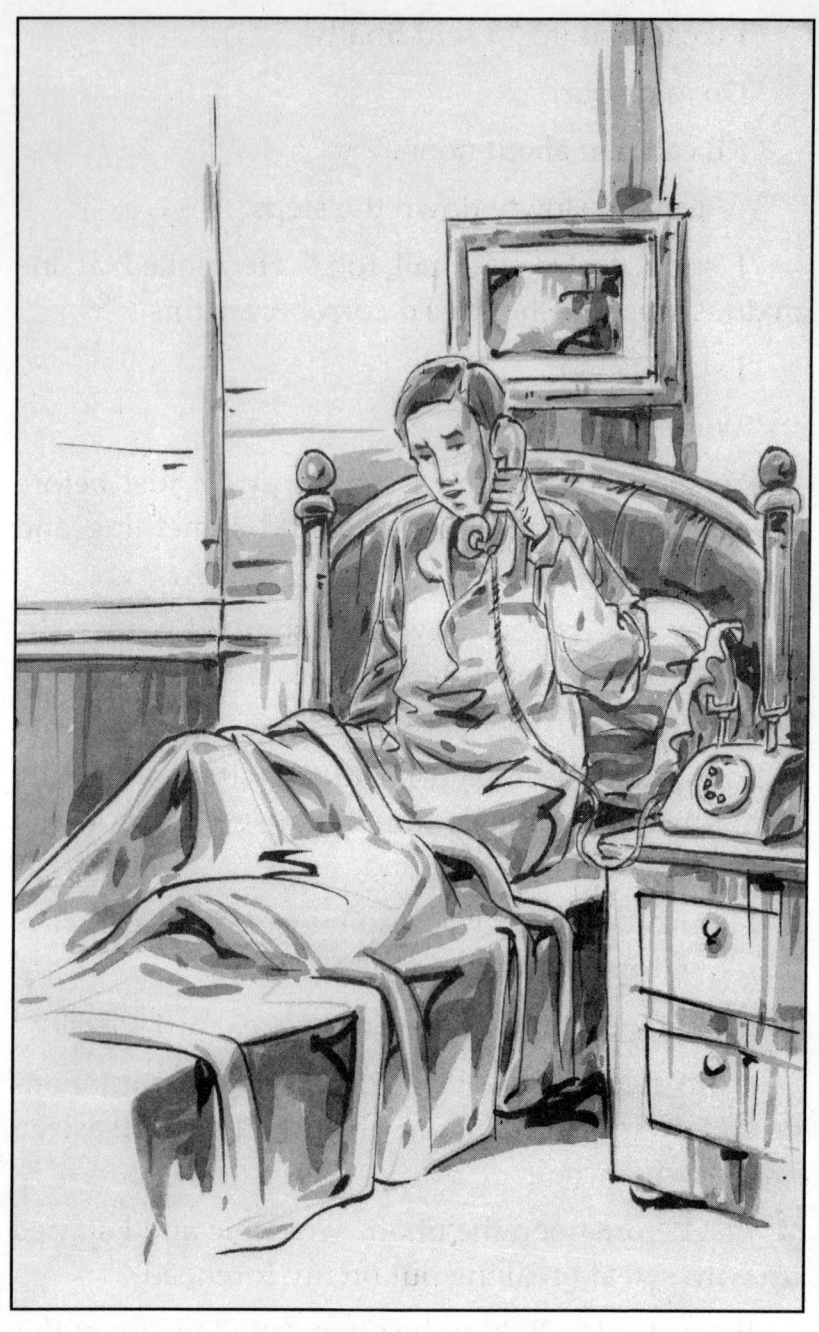

Nick talks to Jordan as he wakes up

between hotels and clubs and private houses made her hard to find in any other way.

Usually her voice came over the wire as something fresh and cool as if a divot from a green golf links had come sailing in at the office window but this morning it seemed harsh and dry.

"I've left Daisy's house," she said. "I'm at Hempstead and I'm going down to Southampton this afternoon."

Probably it had been tactful to leave Daisy's house, but the act annoyed me and her next remark made me rigid.

"You weren't so nice to me last night."

"How could it have mattered then?"

Silence for a moment. Then—

"However—I want to see you."

"I want to see you too."

"Suppose I don't go to Southampton, and come into town this afternoon?"

"No—I don't think this afternoon."

"Very well."

"It's impossible this afternoon. Various——"

We talked like that for a while and then abruptly we weren't talking any longer.

I don't know which of us hung up with a sharp click but I know I didn't care.

I couldn't have talked to her across a tea-table that day if I never talked to her again in this world.

I called Gatsby's house a few minutes later, but the line was busy. I tried four times; finally an exasperated central told me the wire was being kept open for long distance from Detroit.

Taking out my time-table I drew a small circle around the three-fifty train. Then I leaned back in my chair and tried to think. It was just noon.

When I passed the ash heaps on the train that morning I crossed deliberately to the other side of the car.

I suppose there'd be a curious crowd around there all day with little boys searching for dark spots in the dust and some garrulous man telling over and over what happened until it became less and less real even to him and he could tell it no longer and Myrtle Wilson's tragic achievement was forgotten.

Now I want to go back a little and tell what happened at the garage after we left there the night before.

They had difficulty in locating the sister, Catherine. She must have broken her rule against drinking that night for when she arrived she was stupid with liquor and unable to understand that the ambulance had already gone to Flushing.

When they convinced her of this she immediately fainted as if that was the intolerable part of the affair.

Someone kind or curious took her in his car and drove her in the wake of her sister's body.

Until long after midnight a changing crowd lapped up against the front of the garage while George Wilson rocked himself back and forth on the couch inside. For a while the door of the office was open and everyone who came into the garage glanced irresistibly through it.

Finally someone said it was a shame and closed the door. Michaelis and several other men were with him—first four or five men, later two or three men.

About three o'clock the quality of Wilson's incoherent muttering changed—he grew quieter and began to talk about the yellow car.

He announced that he had a way of finding out whom the yellow car belonged to, and then he blurted out that a couple of months ago his wife had come from the city with her face bruised and her nose swollen.

But when he heard himself say this, he flinched and began to cry "Oh, my God!" again in his groaning voice. Michaelis made a clumsy attempt to distract him.

"How long have you been married, George? Come on there, try and sit still a minute and answer my question. How long have you been married?"

"Twelve years."

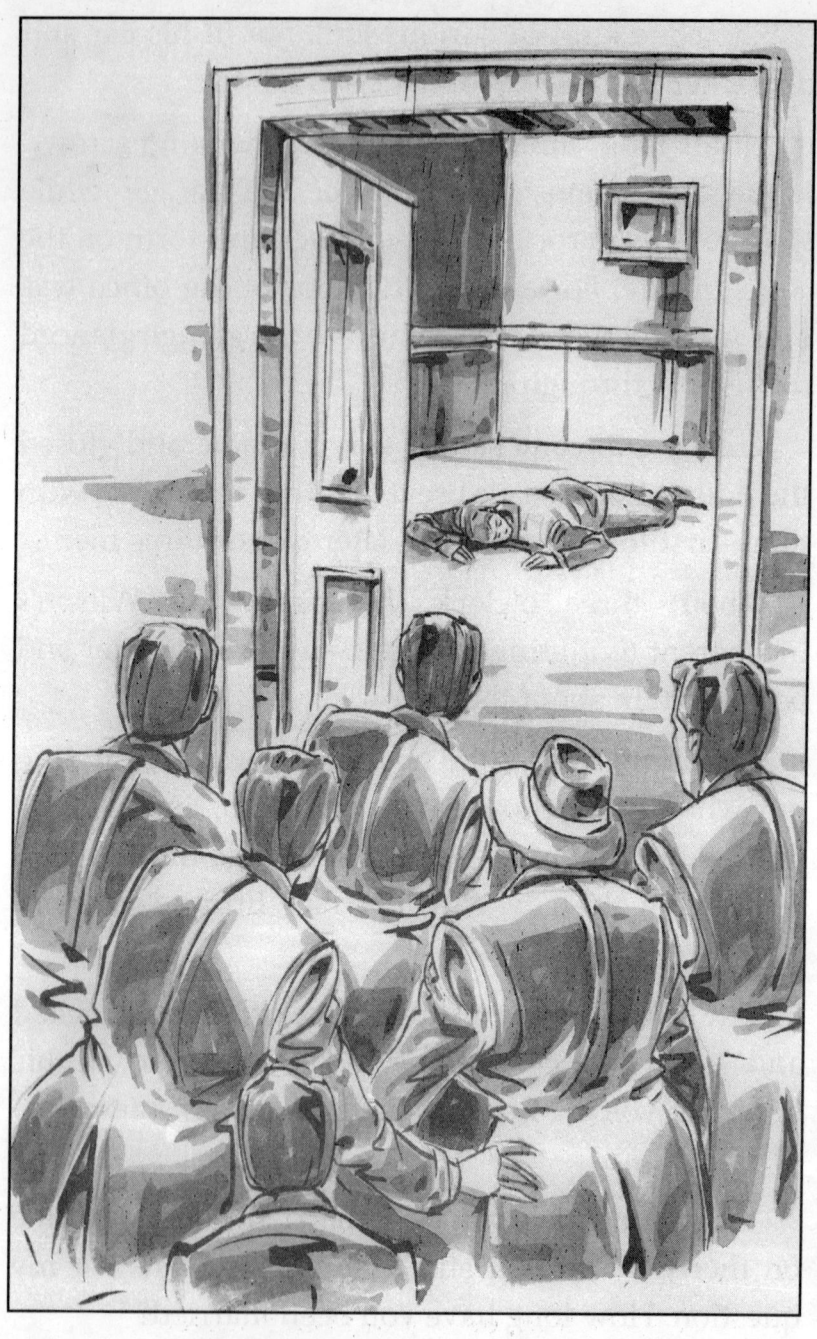

Crowd assembles outside the garage

"Ever had any children? Come on, George, sit still—I asked you a question. Did you ever have any children?"

The hard brown beetles kept thudding against the dull light and whenever Michaelis heard a car go tearing along the road outside it sounded to him like the car that hadn't stopped a few hours before.

"Have you got a church you go to sometimes, George? Maybe even if you haven't been there for a long time? Maybe I could call up the church and get a priest to come over and he could talk to you, see?"

"Don't belong to any."

"You ought to have a church, George, for times like this. You must have gone to church once. Didn't you get married in a church? Listen, George, listen to me. Didn't you get married in a church?"

"That was a long time ago."

The effort of answering broke the rhythm of his rocking—for a moment he was silent. Then the same half knowing, half bewildered look came back into his faded eyes.

"Look in the drawer there," he said, pointing at the desk.

"Which drawer?"

"That drawer—that one."

Michaelis opened the drawer nearest his hand. There was nothing in it but a small expensive dog leash made of leather and braided silver. It was apparently new.

"This?" he inquired, holding it up.

Wilson stared and nodded.

"I found it yesterday afternoon. She tried to tell me about it but I knew it was something funny."

"You mean your wife bought it?"

"She had it wrapped in tissue paper on her bureau."

Michaelis didn't see anything odd in that and he gave Wilson a dozen reasons why his wife might have bought the dog leash. But conceivably

Wilson had heard some of these same explanations before, from Myrtle, because he began saying "Oh, my God!" again in a whisper—his comforter left several explanations in the air.

"Then he killed her," said Wilson. His mouth dropped open suddenly.

"Who did?"

"I have a way of finding out."

"You're morbid, George," said his friend.

"This has been a strain to you and you don't know what you're saying. You'd better try and sit quiet till morning."

"He murdered her."

"It was an accident, George."

Wilson shook his head. His eyes narrowed and his mouth widened slightly with the ghost of a superior "Hm!"

"I know," he said definitely, "I'm one of these trusting fellas and I don't think any harm to NObody, but when I get to know a thing I know it. It was the man in that car. She ran out to speak to him and he wouldn't stop."

Michaelis had seen this too but it hadn't occurred to him that there was any special significance in it. He believed that Mrs. Wilson had been running away from her husband, rather than trying to stop any particular car.

"How could she of been like that?"

"She's a deep one," said Wilson, as if that answered the question. "Ah-h-h——"

He began to rock again and Michaelis stood twisting the leash in his hand.

"Maybe you got some friend that I could telephone for, George?"

This was a forlorn hope—he was almost sure that Wilson had no friend: there was not enough of him for his wife.

"I spoke to her," he muttered, after a long silence. "I told her she might fool me but she couldn't fool God."

Death of Gatsby

Standing behind him Michaelis saw with a shock that he was looking at the eyes of Doctor T. J. Eckleburg which had just emerged pale and enormous from the dissolving night.

"God sees everything," repeated Wilson.

"That's an advertisement," Michaelis assured him. Something made him turn away from the window and look back into the room. But Wilson stood there a long time, his face close to the window pane, nodding into the twilight.

Wilson was quieter now and Michaelis went home to sleep; when he awoke four hours later and hurried back to the garage Wilson was gone.

His movements—he was on foot all the time—were afterward traced to Port

Roosevelt and then to Gad's Hill where he bought a sandwich that he didn't eat and a cup of coffee. By half past two he was in West Egg where he asked someone the way to Gatsby's house. So by that time he knew Gatsby's name.

At two o'clock Gatsby put on his bathing suit and left word with the butler that if any one phoned word was to be brought to him at the pool.

No telephone message arrived but the butler went without his sleep and waited for it until four o'clock—until long after there was any one to give it to if it came. He must have looked up at an unfamiliar sky through frightening leaves and shivered as he found what a grotesque thing a rose is and how raw the sunlight was upon the scarcely created grass. A new world, material without being real, where poor ghosts, breathing dreams like air, drifted fortuitously about . . . like that ashen, fantastic figure gliding toward him through the amorphous trees.

The chauffeur heard the shots—afterward he could only say that he hadn't thought anything much about them. I drove from the station directly to Gatsby's house and my rushing anxiously up the front steps was the first thing that alarmed any one. But they knew then, I firmly believe. With scarcely a word said, four of us, the chauffeur, butler, gardener and I, hurried down to the pool.

There was a faint, barely perceptible movement of the water as the fresh flow from one end urged its way toward the drain at the other.

With little ripples that were hardly the shadows of waves, the laden mattress moved irregularly down the pool. A small gust of wind that scarcely corrugated the surface was enough to disturb its accidental course with its accidental burden. The touch of a cluster of leaves revolved it slowly, tracing, like the leg of compass, a thin red circle in the water.

It was after we started with Gatsby toward the house that the gardener saw Wilson's body a little way off in the grass, and the holocaust was complete.

Chapter 9

After two years I remember the rest of that day, and that night and the next day, only as an endless drill of police and photographers and newspaper men in and out of Gatsby's front door.

Someone with a positive manner, perhaps a detective, used the expression "mad man" as he bent over Wilson's body that afternoon, and the adventitious authority of his voice set the key for the newspaper reports next morning. Most of those reports were a nightmare—grotesque, circumstantial, eager and untrue.

I found myself on Gatsby's side, and alone. From the moment I telephoned news of the catastrophe to West Egg village, every surmise about him, and every practical question, was referred to me.

At first I was surprised and confused; then, as he lay in his house and didn't move or breathe or speak hour upon hour it grew upon me that I was responsible, because no one else was interested.

I called up Daisy half an hour after we found him, called her instinctively and without hesitation. But she and Tom had gone away early that afternoon, and taken baggage with them.

I wanted to get somebody for him. I wanted to go into the room where he lay and reassure him: "I'll get somebody for you, Gatsby. Don't worry.

*Police and photographers and newspaper men
at Gatsby's front door*

Just trust me and I'll get somebody for you——"

Meyer Wolfshiem's name wasn't in the phone book.

The butler gave me his office address on Broadway and I called Information, but by the time I had the number it was long after five and no one answered the phone.

I went back to the drawing room and thought for an instant that they were chance visitors, all these official people who suddenly filled it.

But as they drew back the sheet and looked at Gatsby with unmoved eyes, his protest continued in my brain.

"Look here, old sport, you've got to get somebody for me. You've got to try hard. I can't go through this alone."

Next morning I sent the butler to New York with a letter to Wolfshiem which asked for information and urged him to come out on the next train.

That request seemed superfluous when I wrote it.

I was sure he'd start when he saw the newspapers, just as I was sure there'd be a wire from Daisy before noon—but neither a wire nor Mr. Wolfshiem arrived, no one arrived except more police and photographers and newspaper men.

I think it was on the third day that a telegram signed Henry C. Gatz arrived from a town in Minnesota.

It said only that the sender was leaving immediately and to postpone the funeral until he came.

It was Gatsby's father, a solemn old man very helpless and dismayed, bundled up in a long cheap ulster against the warm September day.

He was on the point of collapse so I took him into the music room and made him sit down while I sent for something to eat.

But he wouldn't eat and the glass of milk spilled from his trembling hand.

"I saw it in the Chicago newspaper," he said. "It was all in the Chicago newspaper. I started right away."

"I didn't know how to reach you."

His eyes, seeing nothing, moved ceaselessly about the room.

"It was a mad man," he said. "He must have been mad."

I took him into the drawing-room, where his son lay, and left him there.

After a little while Mr. Gatz opened the door and came out, his mouth ajar, his face flushed slightly, his eyes leaking isolated and unpunctual tears.

He had reached an age where death no longer has the quality of ghastly surprise, and when he looked around him now for the first time and saw the height and splendor of the hall and the great rooms opening out from it into other rooms his grief began to be mixed with an awed pride.

I helped him to a bedroom upstairs; while he took off his coat and vest I told him that all arrangements had been deferred until he came.

"Look here, this is a book he had when he was a boy. It just shows you."

He opened it at the back cover and turned it around for me to see.

On the last fly-leaf was printed the word SCHEDULE, and the date September 12th, 1906. And underneath:

Rise from bed .... 6.00 A.M.

Dumbbell exercise and wall-scaling ...... 6.15-6.30 "Study electricity, etc .... 7.15-8.15 "

Work .... 8.30-4.30 P.M.

Baseball and sports .... 4.30-5.00 "

Practice elocution, poise and how to attain it 5.00-6.00 "

Study needed inventions .... 7.00-9.00 "

GENERAL RESOLVES

No wasting time at Shafters or [a name, indecipherable]

No more smoking or chewing

Bath every other day

Nick and Mr Gatz

Read one improving book or magazine per week

Save $5.00 [crossed out] $3.00 per week

Be better to parents

"I come across this book by accident," said the old man. "It just shows you, don't it?"

"It just shows you."

"Jimmy was bound to get ahead. He always had some resolves like this or something. Do you notice what he's got about improving his mind? He was always great for that."

He was reluctant to close the book, reading each item aloud and then looking eagerly at me.

I think he rather expected me to copy down the list for my own use.

A little before three the Lutheran minister arrived from Flushing and I began to look involuntarily out the windows for other cars.

So did Gatsby's father. And as the time passed and the servants came in and stood waiting in the hall, his eyes began to blink anxiously and he spoke of the rain in a worried uncertain way.

The minister glanced several times at his watch so I took him aside and asked him to wait for half an hour.

But it wasn't any use. Nobody came.

About five o'clock our procession of three cars reached the cemetery and stopped in a thick drizzle beside the gate—first a motor hearse, horribly black and wet, then Mr. Gatz and the minister and I in the limousine, and, a little later, four or five servants and the postman from West Egg in Gatsby's station wagon, all wet to the skin.

As we started through the gate into the cemetery I heard a car stop and then the sound of someone splashing after us over the soggy ground.

I looked around. It was the man with owl-eyed glasses whom I had found marvelling over Gatsby's books in the library one night three months before.

I'd never seen him since then. I don't know how he knew about the funeral or even his name.

The rain poured down his thick glasses and he took them off and wiped them to see the protecting canvas unrolled from Gatsby's grave.

I tried to think about Gatsby then for a moment but he was already too far away and I could only remember, without resentment, that Daisy hadn't sent a message or a flower.

Dimly I heard someone murmur "Blessed are the dead that the rain falls on," and then the owl-eyed man said "Amen to that," in a brave voice.

We straggled down quickly through the rain to the cars. Owl-Eyes spoke to me by the gate.

"I couldn't get to the house," he remarked.

"Neither could anybody else."

"Go on!" He started. "Why, my God! they used to go there by the hundreds."

He took off his glasses and wiped them again outside and in. "The poor son-of-a-bitch," he said.

When we pulled out into the winter night and the real snow, our snow, began to stretch out beside us and twinkle against the windows, and the dim lights of small Wisconsin stations moved by, a sharp wild brace came suddenly into the air.

We drew in deep breaths of it as we walked back from dinner through the cold vestibules, unutterably aware of our identity with this country for one strange hour before we melted indistinguishably into it again.

That's my middle west—not the wheat or the prairies or the lost Swede towns but the thrilling, returning trains of my youth and the street lamps and sleigh bells in the frosty dark and the shadows of holly wreaths thrown by lighted windows on the snow.

I am part of that, a little solemn with the feel of those long winters, a little complacent from growing up in the Carraway house in a city where dwellings are still called through decades by a family's name.

I see now that this has been a story of the West, after all—Tom and Gatsby, Daisy and Jordan and I, were all Westerners, and perhaps we possessed some deficiency in common which made us subtly unadaptable to Eastern life.

A car stops at the cemetery

Even when the East excited me most, even when I was most keenly aware of its superiority to the bored, sprawling, swollen towns beyond the Ohio, with their interminable inquisitions which spared only the children and the very old—even then it had always for me a quality of distortion.

West Egg especially still figures in my more fantastic dreams. I see it as a night scene by El Greco: a hundred houses, at once conventional and grotesque, crouching under a sullen, overhanging sky and a lustreless moon.

In the foreground four solemn men in dress suits are walking along the sidewalk with a stretcher on which lies a drunken woman in a white evening dress.

Her hand, which dangles over the side, sparkles cold with jewels. Gravely the men turn in at a house—the wrong house. But no one knows the woman's name, and no one cares.

After Gatsby's death the East was haunted for me like that, distorted beyond my eyes' power of correction. So when the blue smoke of brittle leaves was in the air and the wind blew the wet laundry stiff on the line I decided to come back home.

There was one thing to be done before I left, an awkward, unpleasant thing that perhaps had better have been let alone.

But I wanted to leave things in order and not just trust that obliging and indifferent sea to sweep my refuse away.

I saw Jordan Baker and talked over and around what had happened to us together and what had happened afterward to me, and she lay perfectly still listening in a big chair.

She was dressed to play golf and I remember thinking she looked like a good illustration, her chin raised a little, jauntily, her hair the color of an autumn leaf, her face the same brown tint as the fingerless glove on her knee.

When I had finished she told me without comment that she was engaged to another man. I doubted that though there were several she could have married at a nod of her head but I pretended to be surprised.

For just a minute I wondered if I wasn't making a mistake, then I thought it all over again quickly and got up to say goodbye.

"Nevertheless you did throw me over," said Jordan suddenly. "You threw me over on the telephone. I don't give a damn about you now but it was a new experience for me and I felt a little dizzy for a while."

We shook hands.

"Oh, and do you remember—" she added, "——a conversation we had once about driving a car?"

"Why—not exactly."

"You said a bad driver was only safe until she met another bad driver?

Well, I met another bad driver, didn't I? I mean it was careless of me to make such a wrong guess.

I thought you were rather an honest, straightforward person. I thought it was your secret pride."

"I'm thirty," I said. "I'm five years too old to lie to myself and call it honor."

She didn't answer. Angry, and half in love with her, and tremendously sorry, I turned away.

One afternoon late in October I saw Tom Buchanan.

He was walking ahead of me along Fifth Avenue in his alert, aggressive way, his hands out a little from his body as if to fight off interference, his head moving sharply here and there, adapting itself to his restless eyes.

Just as I slowed up to avoid overtaking him he stopped and began frowning into the windows of a jewelry store.

Suddenly he saw me and walked back holding out his hand.

"What's the matter, Nick? Do you object to shaking hands with me?"

"Yes. You know what I think of you."

"You're crazy, Nick," he said quickly. "Crazy as hell. I don't know what's the matter with you."

"Tom," I inquired, "what did you say to Wilson that afternoon?"

He stared at me without a word and I knew I had guessed right about those missing hours.

One afternoon late in October Nick sees Tom Buchanan

I started to turn away but he took a step after me and grabbed my arm.

"I told him the truth," he said. "He came to the door while we were getting ready to leave and when I sent down word that we weren't in he tried to force his way upstairs.

He was crazy enough to kill me if I hadn't told him who owned the car.

His hand was on a revolver in his pocket every minute he was in the house——" He broke off defiantly.

"What if I did tell him? That fellow had it coming to him. He threw dust into your eyes just like he did in Daisy's but he was a tough one.

He ran over Myrtle like you'd run over a dog and never even stopped his car."

There was nothing I could say, except the one unutterable fact that it wasn't true.

"And if you think I didn't have my share of suffering—look here, when I went to give up that flat and saw that damn box of dog biscuits sitting there on the sideboard I sat down and cried like a baby.

By God it was awful——"

I couldn't forgive him or like him but I saw that what he had done was, to him, entirely justified.

It was all very careless and confused.

They were careless people, Tom and Daisy—they smashed up things and creatures and then retreated back into their money or their vast carelessness or whatever it was that kept them together, and let other people clean up the mess they had made. . . .

I shook hands with him; it seemed silly not to, for I felt suddenly as though I were talking to a child. Then he went into the jewelry store to buy a pearl necklace—or perhaps only a pair of cuff buttons—rid of my provincial squeamishness forever.

Gatsby's house was still empty when I left—the grass on his lawn had grown as long as mine.

One of the taxi drivers in the village never took a fare past the entrance gate without stopping for a minute and pointing inside; perhaps it was he who drove Daisy and Gatsby over to East Egg the night of the accident and perhaps he had made a story about it all his own.

I didn't want to hear it and I avoided him when I got off the train.

I spent my Saturday nights in New York because those gleaming, dazzling parties of his were with me so vividly that I could still hear the music and the laughter faint and incessant from his garden and the cars going up and down his drive.

One night I did hear a material car there and saw its lights stop at his front steps.

But I didn't investigate. Probably it was some final guest who had been away at the ends of the earth and didn't know that the party was over.

On the last night, with my trunk packed and my car sold to the grocer, I went over and looked at that huge incoherent failure of a house once more.

On the white steps an obscene word, scrawled by some boy with a piece of brick, stood out clearly in the moonlight and I erased it, drawing my shoe raspingly along the stone.

Then I wandered down to the beach and sprawled out on the sand.

Most of the big shore places were closed now and there were hardly any lights except the shadowy, moving glow of a ferryboat across the Sound.

And as the moon rose higher the inessential houses began to melt away until gradually I became aware of the old island here that flowered once for Dutch sailors' eyes—a fresh, green breast of the new world.

Its vanished trees, the trees that had made way for Gatsby's house, had once pandered in whispers to the last and greatest of all human dreams; for a transitory enchanted moment man must have held his breath in the presence of this continent, compelled into an aesthetic contemplation he neither understood nor desired, face to face for the last time in history with something commensurate to his capacity for wonder.

And as I sat there brooding on the old, unknown world, I thought of

Nick wanders down to the beach

Gatsby's wonder when he first picked out the green light at the end of

Daisy's dock. He had come a long way to this blue lawn and his dream must have seemed so close that he could hardly fail to grasp it.

He did not know that it was already behind him, somewhere back in that vast obscurity beyond the city, where the dark fields of the republic rolled on under the night.

Gatsby believed in the green light, the orgastic future that year by year recedes before us.

It eluded us then, but that's no matter—tomorrow we will run faster, stretch out our arms farther. . . . And one fine morning——

So we beat on, boats against the current, borne back ceaselessly into the past.

Post-Reading Activities

1. Explain how Fitzgerald uses setting to emphasize the differences between the social classes.

2. Compare and contrast the characters of Tom and Gatsby.

3. Discuss the significance of the title of the novel.

4. What makes Gatsby "great"?

5. What are some of The Great Gatsby's most important symbols?

6. How does Gatsby represent the American dream?

7. Throughout the story, Gatsby has difficulty accepting that the past is over. Where do you find evidence of his trying to recapture the past?